Before he'd had a chance to second-guess himself the words were tumbling out. 'Georgie, wait. I'll do it.'

Her voice was small and he could hear the pain, and yet deep down there was some hope as she turned to face him. 'Do what?'

'I'll be the donor.'

'You?' She wagged her finger—fast. 'Oh, no. No. No. No. Not happening.'

'Unless you have a particular aversion to my DNA? If I was to look objectively I'd say I was pretty okay. I'm a doctor—so not dumb. I'm funny—always a winner.' He pointed to his abs for effect. 'And pretty much the most devastatingly good-looking man in town.'

The sarcasm melted away and the laugh was pure Georgie. 'Yeah, right. That's objective? Don't get above yourself. For one, you have a slightly crooked nose.'

'Rugby injury—not genetic. Besides, you can hardly see it.'

She cocked her hip to one side as she perused him. 'You have particularly broad shoulders.'

'Great for tackling and giving great hugs.'

'On the other hand you do have long legs...' Her voice cracked a little as her gaze scanned his trousers. Her pupils did a funny widening thing. Two red spots appeared on her cheeks. 'Ahem...and big feet.'

'And we all know what that means.' He winked.

'Oh, yeah? No girl wants big feet. Bad for shoe-buying.' She gave him a final once-over glance. Then her voice softened. 'Really, it's a lovely offer, and I'd be stupid not to take you up on it, but what about you? You don't want this. You *really* don't want this.'

'Yes, but you do, Georgie.'

A lifelong reader of most genres, **Louisa George** discovered romance novels later than most, but immediately fell in love with the intensity of emotion, the high drama and the family focus of Mills & Boon® Medical Romance™.

With a Bachelors Degree in Communication and a nursing qualification under her belt, writing medical romance seemed a natural progression and the perfect combination of her two interests. And making things up is a great way to spend the day!

An English ex-pat, Louisa now lives north of Auckland, New Zealand, with her husband, two teenage sons and two male cats. Writing romance is her opportunity to covertly inject a hefty dose of pink into her heavily testosterone-dominated household. When she's not writing or researching Louisa loves to spend time with her family and friends, enjoys travelling and adores great food. She's also hopelessly addicted to Zumba®.

A BABY ON HER CHRISTMAS LIST

BY
LOUISA GEORGE

MILLS & BOON

First published in Great Britain 2014
by Mills & Boon, an imprint of Harlequin (UK) Limited,
Large Print edition 2015
Eton House, 18-24 Paradise Road,
Richmond, Surrey, TW9 1SR

© 2014 Louisa George

ISBN: 978-0-263-25482-2

Harlequin (UK) Limited's policy is to use papers that
are natural, renewable and recyclable products and made
from wood grown in sustainable forests. The logging
and manufacturing processes conform to the legal
environmental regulations of the country of origin.

Printed and bound in Great Britain
by CPI Antony Rowe, Chippenham, Wiltshire

Dedication

To Iona Jones, Sue MacKay, Barbara DeLeo,
Kate David and Nadine Taylor, my gorgeous
Blenheim girls—thank you for the great weekend
at the cottage and your amazing help
to brainstorm this book.

You guys definitely know how to
rock a writing retreat. xx

CHAPTER ONE

Nine months ago...

'I'VE FOUND A baby daddy!' Georgie's wide grin shone brighter than the Southern Cross, her dark brown eyes sparkling even in the bar's dim light.

Liam watched, dumbfounded, as excitement rolled off her, so intense it was almost tangible.

'Well, not a daddy as such. I should really stop saying that. But I have found someone who would be perfect to donate his sperm…which I know makes you shudder, so I'm sorry for saying The Word.' She gave Liam a wicked wink that was absolutely at odds with this whole one-sided conversation.

Whoa.

Too gobsmacked to speak, Liam indicated to her to sit. She tossed her silk wrap and bag on the back of a chair, put her drink down on the table and plonked in the seat opposite him at the only free table in Indigo's crowded lounge.

A baby?

He felt the frown forming and couldn't control it—even if he'd wanted to—and finally found his voice. 'Hey, back right up, missy. Am I dreaming here? I thought you just said something about a baby...'

It had been too long since he'd seen her looking so happy so he was wary about bursting her bubble—but, hell, he was going to burst it anyway. Because that's what real friends did—they talked sense. Just like she'd done the first time they'd met, in the sluice room of the ER; he a lowly med student, losing his cool at the sight of a lifeless newborn, she a student nurse with more calm and control and outright guts than anyone he'd ever met. She'd let him shake, allowed him five minutes to stress out, then had forced him back into the ER to help save the kid's life. And they'd been pretty much glued at the hip ever since.

So he needed to be honest. He raised his voice over the thump-thump-thump of the bar's background bass that usually fuelled their regular Friday night drinking session, but tonight the noise was irritating and obnoxious. 'I go away for three months and come back to sheer madness. What happened to the *Nothing's going to get in the way of those renovations this time? I'm on the real estate ladder now and going up.* What the hell, Geo? A baby? Since when was that on your to-do list?'

Stabbing the ice in her long glass with a straw, she looked up at him, eyes darker now, and he caught a yearning he'd seen glimpses of over the last ten years. She thought she hid it well, but sometimes, when she was distracted or excited, she let her tough guard slip. 'You, of all people, know I've always wanted a family, Liam. It may not have been at the top of my list because I always believed it would just happen at some point. But I can't keep putting it off and leaving it to chance, because chance isn't going my way. And I refuse to prioritise decorating over having a baby. That would be stupid.'

In his opinion, having a baby was right up at the top of stupid but he kept that to himself. And, for the record, it wasn't just decorating—her house needed knock-down-and-start-again renovations. 'But what's the hurry? You're only twenty-eight. It will happen, you've got plenty of time. You just need to find the right guy.' And why that made him shudder more than the *sperm* word, he didn't know.

She let the straw go, then pulled a hair tie from her wrist and curled her long wavy hair into a low ponytail. Her hair was the same colour as caramel, with little streaks of honey and gold. He didn't need to get any closer to know that it smelt like apples or fruit or something vaguely edible. And clearly he'd been away too long if he was starting to notice stuff like that.

Luckily she was oblivious to him staring at her hair and thinking about its colour and smell. 'Oh, yes, and the candidates for husband are queuing up at the door, aren't they? You may have noticed that the pickings for Mr Perfect are slim and slimming further by the day in Auckland. There's a man drought. It's official apparently, New Zealand has a lot fewer men than women my age. Why do you think I've needed you to...*expedite* a few dates for me?' Her shoulders slumped. 'I know we've had fun setting each other up with potentials over the years, but I'm starting to think that—'

'That maybe you're too...picky?' He raised his glass to her. 'Hey, I don't know, but perhaps you could consider only having a one-page check-box list that potentials need to tick, instead of fifteen?'

Her eyes widened as she smiled. 'Get out of here. It is nowhere near fifteen.'

'Not on paper, no. But in your head it is. I've seen you in action, remember. *He's not funny enough. Too intense. Just a joker. Doesn't take me seriously. Just wanted a one-nighter.*' Truth was, Liam had been secretly pretty damned proud she'd spurned most of his mates' advances and that she'd ended most flings before they'd got serious. There was something special about Georgie and she deserved a special kind of bloke. He hadn't met one yet that would be worthy of her.

'So I have standards. I'd settle for Mr *Almost* Perfect if he existed—which he doesn't. I'm getting too short on time.' Her red, loose-fitting summer dress moved softly as she shrugged delicate shoulders. 'I don't know about you, but I get the feeling that asking a man to father your children on a first date might just scare him off.'

'Well, hell, if I asked a man to father my children on any date it'd either be in a nightmare or because I was hallucinating.'

She rolled her eyes. 'You know very well what

I mean. And, yes, you are the straightest guy I've ever met.' Her eyes ran over his chest, lingering a little over his pecs, throat, mouth. Why he noticed he didn't know. And, even stranger, he felt a little hot. When her gaze met his she gave him her usual friendly smile. 'You're looking mighty fit these days, Dr MacAllister. How was Pakistan?'

'Hot, wet and desperate.' As with all his aid missions, he didn't want to relive what he had seen. Enough that he had those images in his own head, without sharing details with others.

'But at least you know you were doing good out there. What were the conditions like? Are you okay? How are you feeling? When do you leave again? Please be happy for me.'

This was always how it was with Georgie: random conversation detours and finishing each other's sentences. But things generally flowed and they knew each other so well that often they didn't have to speak to communicate. So with the sudden baby daddy bombshell he'd never felt so excluded from her life. 'I'm fine. Knackered, but fine, looking forward to a few weeks' locuming at the General's ER. At least there's running water and reliable electricity. And I have a decent bed to sleep in. The next planned rollout for me is in South Sudan in a couple of months.'

'But if they need you earlier...'

He nodded. 'Sure. It's the way it is.'

'I still don't know how you manage all that to-ing and fro-ing. Here a couple of months, then gone again. I like staying in one place.'

And he didn't. The longest he ever stayed anywhere was when he came back here because he needed a semi-permanent job to help fund his aid work. 'But I'm never going away again if it means I come back to crazyville baby talk.'

'It's not crazyville.' Again with the eye roll. He didn't even have to look. This time it was accompanied by an irritated shake of her head. 'I've made a decision to do this now. On my own. I know it'll be tough and it's not the perfect image I've always had in my head about a mum and dad and two point four kids, but that's too far out of reach right now. I've had to curtail my dreaming and get real. Being a solo mum is just fine.'

She stopped talking to take a long drink of what looked a lot like lemonade. On a Friday night? Could be that she was actually serious about this. 'I want to conceive and carry to term, and have a baby…*my* baby…and, if things work out, have another one too. But that's probably greedy and selfish.'

'You deserve to be, Geo, after what you've been through.' *But now? Why now?*

'So, I'm looking forward, and taking an opportunity. Endo is a lot less active during pregnancy so if I could manage two pregnancies in quick succession…if the IUI works, that is… IVF would be a whole different ball game.'

Trying to keep up he lifted his palms towards her. 'IUI? IVF? Slow down a bit. So you're not thinking turkey baster? Or just plain old-fashioned sex? That is a relief.'

'Believe me, I'll do whatever's necessary.'

He didn't doubt it. And finally the reality was sinking in. She was going to do the one thing he'd sworn never to do—and because he was her friend she'd expect him to be supportive. 'So what tipped you over to the dark side?'

And, yes, his reaction would not be what she wanted, but: a) he couldn't help it and; b) he wasn't prepared to lie just to make her feel better. It was precisely because of their friendship that he knew he could be straight up with her.

'You are such a grump. For me there is no dark side. Being abandoned at two days old and having literally no one from then on in has made me want to feel part of something...a family. You know that. I just want what everyone else has, Liam—to feel loved, to be loved. To love. And I have no doubt that there will be some hard times, but I will never leave my baby on a doorstep for someone else to find, and condemn them to a life of foster-homes and social services, like my mum did to me. I will cherish any child I have. I've had my share of dark sides and being pregnant and a mother isn't one of them.'

Her nose wrinkled as she reached across and lightly punched him on the arm. 'So, I was worried things were getting worse endo-wise, so I asked Malcolm to run some more tests at work a few weeks ago.' Her hands palmed across her abdomen—subconsciously? Possibly. Protective? Definitely.

'You've been having more pain? Oh, God, I'm sorry, Georgie. That sucks. Really, I thought you were managing okay.' Liam hated that. Hated that even though he fixed people up every day he didn't have the answers to Georgie's problems and that they were running out of solutions as time ticked on. His heart thumped in sync with the music, hard and loud in his chest. 'What did he say?'

'That the endometriosis is indeed getting worse. That everything in there's getting blocked up and scarred and it won't be long before I'll need pretty major surgery. That it's only a matter of time before pregnancy is going to be nigh on impossible. At least, without a whole lot of effort and money and no promises at the end.'

Her eyes filled with tears. Which, for Georgie, was such a rarity Liam sat there like a useless lump and watched in horror, unable to move. She was the strongest woman he knew. She'd faced tough battles her whole life and she never tired of fighting. No matter how ridiculous her plan sounded, his heart twisted to see her hurting. 'You know how much I need this, Liam. I thought you'd understand. I thought you'd support me. You know, like good friends do? I've been there for you regardless and I kind of hoped you'd feel the same.' Her hand reached for her gut again. 'This idea? This is a good thing.'

It was the worst thing he'd ever heard. 'And so

who is going to provide the...?' He couldn't bring himself to say the word. For an accomplished medic he had trouble imagining what went on behind closed doors at the IVF clinic.

'Sperm? I've decided I'm going to ask Malcolm.'

'What?' Liam almost choked on his beer. 'Your boss?'

'And that's wrong, why? He's smart. Not unattractive. Owns a successful IVF clinic and has helped thousands of women achieve their dreams, so he's compassionate too. Those are all the right kind of genes I'd look for in a father for my child.'

'He's still also your boss.'

She hip-planted both hands. 'And I'm pretty sure he'd want to help. He sees this kind of thing every day, so to him it's not an unusual request. I'll ask him to sign a contract to keep things simple. I have enough money put by to keep me going for a while and the clinic has agreed to reduce my hours after maternity leave.'

Maternity leave. Contracts. That sounded far from simple. And the money she had put by was supposed to be for renovations to help her become more financially independent. 'Seems like you have it all figured out.'

'He knows how much I want this. How much I need to know DNA and family history. It's been my life's dream. Just a little…*expedited*.' She gave him a smile at their shared joke.

Liam didn't feel much like laughing. Sure, she'd talked about this on and off over the years but now the reality hit him in the gut like a two-ton truck. She wanted a baby. A family. Kids. 'Surely asking your boss is downright unprofessional. Unethical.'

'A friend helping a friend? Since when did that cross any kind of line?'

'Where would you like me to start?' It crossed more lines than Liam cared to think of. It would be like…like if he offered to father her child. Ridiculous. Ludicrous.

Wouldn't it?

The thought flitted across a corner of his mind. He pushed it away. Ludicrous indeed.

'Malcolm saw how upset I was at the results.' As she spoke she seemed to loosen up a little. Determined, but calm. 'I've asked to have a meeting with him next week. If he says no then I'll have a rethink.'

'It sounds messy to me. How about using one of the anonymous donors at the clinic? You get to know about their family history, too. You can choose anyone that ticks your fifteen pages of boxes.' He didn't know why someone anonymous fathering her child seemed like a better option. It just *felt* better. A long way from right, but better. 'And why didn't you ask me?'

What the hell?

He didn't even know where that question had come from. As she stared at him his chest tightened.

'Is that what this is all about? You're upset because I didn't ask you? Honestly? The man who comes out in hives when he even sees a baby?' As soon as the words left her mouth she closed her eyes and pressed her lips together. Too late. After a beat or two she slowly opened her eyes again and winced. 'Oh, my God, I'm sorry. Really. I'm sorry, Liam. I am. I didn't mean…I'm so sorry. But I just know how you feel about families.'

'Do you?'

She looked surprised at his question. Probably because he'd kept his past to himself and never spoke about what he wanted for the future. But families and babies were something he definitely had an aversion to. No, not an aversion, just a deep desire not to go there. Ever.

Her voice softened. 'Since you always refuse to talk about anything deeper than what you had for lunch, I have to surmise. You have a track record of emotional avoidance. So I've always assumed that big loving, meddling, messy, happy families aren't something on your wish list. In all honesty, you'd be the last person I'd ask. And, judging by your current reaction, I think I'm right.'

Liam's face was all shadows and hollows. His blue eyes had darkened to navy. Only once before had Georgie seen him look so utterly haunted, and that had been the day they'd met and she'd forced him to work on that newborn.

Later that night, when they'd gone for the first of many subsequent beers, the alcohol had made his tongue loose and he'd mentioned a family tragedy involving his sister, Lauren. But then had clammed up so tight Georgie had never been able to open him up to that particular hotspot conversation again. And since then he'd absorbed whatever it was that had thrown him off balance that day. Until now.

His voice was low when he eventually spoke. 'I just think you could have talked to me about it all first. Put more thought into it.'

'I don't think that's possible, it's all I've been thinking about for weeks, turning scenarios over and over in my head.' She watched as anger and hurt twitched through him until he wrestled it under control. Why couldn't he just smile and pat her hand and say what a brilliant idea it was? Her words had obviously been a low blow. She'd always respected that he had his reasons for not wanting a family, even if he'd never really fronted up and explained why.

Some support would have been nice, but hadn't she heard this kind of story so many times at work? Babies, IVF and the sometimes desperate journey towards parenthood made strong couples stronger and weak ones fall apart.

Then thank God she and Liam weren't a couple because, judging by this conversation, they'd fall at the first hurdle.

He was her friend, her closest friend in lots of ways; she always took his advice, always went to him with problems. And now she was all kinds of confused, needing time to think and reaffirm.

She stood to leave. 'Look, this was clearly a mistake. I'm going to go home so we can both take some time out. I'm sorry if I've ruined our Friday night. But, you know, I don't know where we'd go from here. Trying to play your wingman and find a date for you with some poor unsuspecting woman just isn't my idea of fun right now.'

He tipped his glass towards her again, but he didn't get up. Didn't try to make her feel better. And he always tried to make her feel better.

Which was why his opposition was spooking her more than she'd anticipated. Still, she'd made this decision and she was sticking with it.

She had no choice. This was her life. Her chance.

And to hell with him if he wasn't going to be there right when she needed it most. She threw her wrap round her shoulders. 'I'll...I don't know... see you later?'

He watched her stand. He still didn't move but his voice was more controlled as he gave her a small smile. 'Heaven help us all when you start taking the hormone injections.'

'Oh? Why?'

'Aren't they supposed to make you all antsy and volatile?'

'What?' She couldn't bring herself to tell him she'd been taking them already. And, yes, she was being antsy. But it was his reaction that had made her like that, not the medications. 'Maybe, just maybe you have royally pissed me off. And to add insult to injury, you're now being condescending. Patronising.'

'Just honest. As always.' Yes, she supposed he was. One of things she relied on him for was his frank honesty. 'So when is it all happening? The impregnating thing?'

'So very clinical, Liam.'

'Yes. Isn't it?'

'I was hoping it would be in the next couple of weeks if possible.'

The glass in his hand hit the table with a crash. 'What? So soon? You don't mess around, do you? You don't want to talk a bit more? At least listen to someone else's opinion?'

'And have you try to convince me against it? I don't think so. I don't need your negativity. It's a chance, Liam. I need to take it.'

For a few seconds he looked at her. Just stared at her. She couldn't read him. The man she'd thought she knew pretty much inside and out, and she couldn't even guess what he was thinking.

After a torturous silence that seemed to increase the tension tenfold, he spoke, 'Yes. Yes, you do. Take the chance, Geo.' Now he stood up and walked her to the door. Once outside he didn't wrap her in his usual goofy bear hug. Didn't graze her cheek with a kiss and a smile. Didn't give her a wink and make her laugh. 'Let me know how you get on.'

'Why? So you can make me doubt myself all over again?'

He took her by the shoulders and his gaze bored into her. 'Because I'm your friend, Georgie.'

And then she ached for him to give her one of his hugs more than anything else in the world. But he turned away. Back towards the bar and the white noise that seemed to be mingling with his words and filling her head with doubts.

What if he was right? What if this was the far side of crazy? What the hell did she know about family anyway? About parenting? It wasn't as if she'd had any experience on either side of that particular fence. What if Malcolm didn't follow through? What if he did?

Worse, what if this rift meant that the friendship she had with Liam would be broken for ever? He was the closest thing she had to any notion of family, and the thought of not having him in her life made her suddenly feel empty and cold.

Torn and confused, she climbed into a waiting cab and watched him retreat to the bar, his dark T-shirt straining across well-defined broad shoulders, and a gait that screamed defiance.

And what the hell was going on with those pecs? The man had suddenly developed muscles of steel. Strange, too, that in the midst of all this turmoil she should even notice. That, and the shape of his lips, the way his mouth curved and softened as he smiled, which had been rare but welcome tonight. Those hormones were clearly playing havoc with her head.

But judging by the sudden strange slick of heat that hit her breasts and abdomen—which surely must be a reaction to the muggy Auckland evening—they were messing with her body too.

CHAPTER TWO

Mum's had a stroke. Had to go back to UK. Don't know for how long. Will keep you in the loop. Sorry. Can we have that meeting when I get back?

SHUTTING THE IVF clinic room door, so she could have a moment to take it all in, Georgie stared at the text, her gut clenching. Bile rose to the back of her throat. She felt dizzy.

And downright selfish.

Inhaling deeply, she pulled herself together. For goodness' sake, it wasn't the end of the world, just the end of an opportunity. That was all. There would be another chance, next month or the month after. Some time. With a different donor.

She should be feeling sorry for her boss, not herself.

No worries, Malcolm. Safe journey. Sending hugs for your mum x

And yet she felt as if her world was closing in on her, that she was fast running out of time and her dream was getting further out of reach. Scrolling through her texts, she found her conversation thread with Liam and started to type. Then stopped. She hadn't heard a thing from him for four days, and even though she knew he'd be busy, catching up on everything at work, she felt a little lost. Normally he'd text her with funny stories from his shift, jokes, stuff. Just stuff. But ever since Friday she'd been hit by silence. And it hurt a little that he knew what she was going through but didn't want to see how she was doing.

Okay, it hurt a lot.

So maybe that would be the norm from now on. She didn't want to think about that. But for the last few days it hadn't been just his absence that had been on her mind. It had been that crazy tingly feeling that had swept through her body the other night, just looking at him. And then an out-of-proportion feeling of loss that he wasn't being supportive. It was absurd. Seemed those meds made her overreact in lots of different ways.

The clinic room phone interrupted her thoughts and brought her back to reality. 'Georgie speaking.'

It was Helen, the receptionist, and Georgie's good friend. 'I have a patient here, Kate Holland. Says she doesn't feel too great. Can you see her straight away?'

'Kate? Sure, I remember her, she was in just the other day. I'll be right through.' Helen rarely showed any kind of emotion, so the anxiety in her voice made Georgie take notice. Putting her own worries aside, she made sure the clinic couch was ready, opened up Kate's notes on the laptop then collected her patient, who appeared noticeably short of breath, flushed and anxious.

'Kate. What's the problem? Are you okay?'

'No. I feel pretty rubbish, actually. My stomach hurts and I'm so thirsty.' For a toned and fit marathon runner Kate climbed onto the bed with a lot of effort.

Alarm bells began to ring. Georgie settled the young woman against the pillow, silently counting the laboured respiratory rate. 'You've been having the injections, right? Any other problems? Nausea? Vomiting?'

Kate nodded. 'Yes. Twice this morning and I feel really sick now. But so thirsty.'

Georgie took her patient's hand and measured

her pulse. Fast and thready. Any number of scenarios raced through her mind. Fertility drugs had a tranche of usually mild and temporary side-effects, but when they were severe they could be life-threatening. 'Peeing okay? If you can do us a sample, that'd be great.'

'Not much at all. But I'll try.'

'Okay, when you next need to go, yell out.' Giving Kate a quick examination and piecing together her patient's history, Georgie reached a preliminary diagnosis. It wasn't what either she or her patient wanted to hear. 'How long have you felt like this?'

'The past couple of days or so. I started feeling really sick yesterday.' Kate gripped Georgie's hand, her flushed face tight and scared. 'But please don't tell me we have to stop the injections. Please say we can do this. It's our last chance.'

Georgie gently encouraged her to lie back down, not wanting to upset her even more but realising that time was of the essence. 'I know, Kate. I know. But don't get ahead of yourself. I'll quickly get the doctor to come check you over, he'll probably suggest you have a short stay in hospital, just a few days or so, to check everything's okay...'

After the doctor had confirmed Kate's diagnosis, Georgie arranged the next few steps. 'Because you're publicly funded, we'll transfer you to the General Hospital gynae ward, that's the closest to your home. They'll look after you. I promise.'

'What about the IVF? Will that happen now?'

Georgie took her hand again. 'Sweetheart, you remember the doctor saying you had something called OHSS? That's our medical shorthand for ovarian hyper-stimulation syndrome. That means your body has reacted very strongly to the drugs. You have too much fluid in your abdomen, which is why you're out of breath. You're dehydrated, but we need to watch how much fluid you drink because we don't want you overloaded. You have a swollen red calf, which might mean you have a blood clot. We've arranged for some scans and a few more tests at the hospital. You need to rest and let your body heal before you do any more.'

'We can't afford any more. This is it, our last chance. Mark will be so disappointed. He's been really positive this time round, we both have. We talked about a Christmas baby, he got so excited. He wants to be a dad so much.' Fat tears rolled down Kate's red cheeks and Georgie's heart melted.

Some people, such as Kate, were lucky enough to be eligible for publicly funded treatment for a limited number of cycles. Having already waited for months and had one failed attempt, this was indeed Kate's last chance. She and her husband Mark had a low income and there was no way could they afford the high costs and even more time off work for private IVF. Life was so unfair sometimes.

Georgie dealt with these scenarios in her job every day, and she'd always managed to keep a professional emotional distance, but today it felt deeply personal. She knew how desperate it was to have a ticking clock. And a chance that could be blown for any random reason. 'We'll do the best we can for you, Kate.' But she wouldn't make any promises. It wasn't her style to give her patients false hope, no matter how much her heart ached in sync with them. 'In the meantime, you have to get better.'

If anything, it made Georgie more determined to grab her chance as soon as she could. Deciding to go through with it was the first step on what she knew was going to be a long road. She had no illusions as to the prospect of being a single pregnant woman, then a solo mother. It would be immensely rewarding. It would be hard. And with no one else to help shoulder the burden she knew there would be times she'd find it difficult to cope. But she would. She'd been on her own her whole life. She didn't need anyone else. But needing and wanting were two different things.

On days like these she'd usually ring Liam and have a whinge. Often he'd suggest a drink or a movie or something to cheer her up. But as he'd gone AWOL and she didn't fancy another grim conversation, she'd do things differently tonight. He certainly wasn't the only friend she had in the world.

'Okay, that's me over and out. See you in the morning,' Liam called to his secretary, then grabbed his work bag and made his way through the crowded ER to the exit. It had been one hell of a day, dealing with staff shortages, bus-crash casualties and the usual walk-ins. What he needed now was a sundowner at the local and an early night.

The hospital doors swept open and he took his

first breath of fresh air for eleven hours. It was tinged with a familiar fragrance that had him turning his head. She was standing way over to his left, half-hidden by a tall confident-looking man, and Liam would have missed her and walked by if he hadn't caught that sweet, flowery scent.

For some reason, as he saw her deep in conversation with a stranger, his heart hammered. Mainly, he suspected, because he'd bawled her out the other day and hadn't had the chance to make things right. 'Georgie. Hi. What are you doing here?'

She whirled round, her cheeks reddening, her green nursing scrubs making her look younger somehow. Vulnerable, which she'd hate. There was a ripple of tension as her shoulders straightened, but she masked it. 'Oh. Hey. I'm dropping off a patient's bag. She had to be admitted unexpectedly and left it at the clinic by mistake. This is her husband, Mark.'

'Liam. Hi, I work here.' As he shook hands with the guy the heart-hammering slowed a little. Was it wrong to feel relief that his friend wasn't sick, but that another man's wife was? Damn right it was. But relief shuddered through him anyway. 'Is everything okay?'

'Mark's wife, Kate, has OHSS, so she's feeling a bit fragile. Mark's on his way up to see her on Ward Three.'

'Ah, yes. I remember seeing her name on the admissions board. She'll be okay, mate. She's in good hands.'

The man nodded grimly and headed through the main entrance. Leaving just Liam and Georgie and a weird sense of displacement. Georgie played with the handle of her handbag, looked at her feet. 'I should probably go.'

Not without some kind of resolution, he thought grimly. This was painful. They'd never had this kind of weird, tense scenario play out before. 'Wait. Are you okay?'

What he meant was, *Are we okay?*

'Yes. Thanks. You?' She raised her head and looked at him. She looked tired, drawn. The edges of her eyes were ringed with black. Which was a far cry from the last time he'd seen her when she'd been brimful of excitement, and he'd stomped all over her happy mood. Was the dark look just for him or had something else happened to her?

Okay, stop guessing and cut the crap. 'Look, Geo, I didn't mean to pee all over your parade. I'm sorry about the other night. I was tired and just caught by surprise.'

'Clearly. And you've been too busy to send a text?' But the iron-clad barriers seemed to give just a little with his apology. 'Or did they get lost in cyberspace, along with your good manners?'

'As it happens, things have been manic here. I've done four long days with the last vestiges of jet-lag messing with my brain.' She didn't need to hear all that. 'I did think about texting you more than a few times. But I wasn't sure whether you'd slap me or eye-stab me with one of those killer looks you save for especially annoying people that drive you mad on purpose. And I wasn't up to taking the risk.'

That, at least, got a smile. 'Aw, Liam, I'd never eye-stab you. How could you say such a thing?'

'I know what you're capable of, my girl. Down-right scary at times.' He walked with her towards the car park, feeling a little more relaxed. 'Er... done the deed yet?'

'By which you mean the assisted fertility?' Georgie slowed and gave him what he had come to recognise as one of her false smiles. Her mouth flipped up into the usual grin, but her eyes didn't shine. In fact, nothing about her was shining tonight. Even her *caramel* hair—it was just plain weird that he'd started to notice things that he'd always glossed over—seemed dulled. 'Malcolm's had to go away due to a family crisis, so I've put off asking him.'

'Oh. I see.' And with that news he really should have been cock-a-hoop but he wasn't. Strange emotions rippled through him, mainly disappointment for her. It was what she wanted. She'd been so excited and determined the other day, to the point that he'd been unable to talk any sense into her.

Now she looked like she needed bolstering. 'Okay. So you've got plenty of time. I'm sure you'll be fine waiting just a little while longer. Have you had any thoughts about asking anyone else? What about the donor lists?'

She frowned. 'Yes, well, it's far from ideal. And, like I said, time is something I don't have a lot of.'

'You sound like you're waiting for the guillotine or something. Just a touch dramatic, Geo?'

'You think so?' As they closed in on her car

they stopped. She pointed up to the second floor of the hospital with a taut finger that was definitely capable of eye-stabbing if she so wished. 'That lady in there has been trying to get pregnant for five years. And nothing. Zilch. Nil. She's had one chance at IVF, which came up with disappointment, and now everything's on hold until she gets better from the side effects of trying to stimulate her ovaries. I expect that if she gets the go-ahead again she'll have to pay megabucks... and even then it might not work for her.

'I do not want to be that lady, possibly looking at years of pressure and stress. I've got to start the ball rolling and damn well soon. Otherwise when and if I'm finally in a committed relationship with someone who loves me, it might be too late. I have a window of opportunity in my cycle coming up very soon. And I'm disappointed that I can't take advantage of it. Dramatic? If you say so. But, then, you're not the one staring down the barrel of a ticking time bomb.'

'Wow. See? Scary.' He stepped back. 'I'll just make sure I'm out of eye-stabbing range.'

She stalked off to her car, then stopped abruptly and turned on him, gravel scraping underfoot.

Never before had he seen such passion and anger and determination and spirit in anyone. 'For once in your life, Liam, take me seriously.'

'I do. All the time. I was just trying to make you feel better.'

'Well, you didn't. You know what? I bet we could spend the next few weeks going round in circles with this and you'd never understand.'

Oh, he understood all right. He'd been thinking about it for days, ever since she'd brought the subject up. In fact, that ludicrous idea that had flitted through his head had taken seed and would not let go.

But the ramifications were huge.

She glared at him, her eyes fierce, curls springing loose and free around her face. Her mouth taut and determined. She looked magnificent and terrifying, like the time she'd pushed him into Resus for that baby. And many times since when she'd been hell-bent on partying hard or just grasping life in her hands and making the most of it. She'd been like that since he'd known her—reaching, grasping, dreaming. Making her life full, taking what she wanted. Because she'd had so little for so long she hadn't wanted to waste a moment, and she defied anyone who stood in her way.

She was strong and staunch and loyal and in that second he knew that if *his* back was against the wall, she'd do anything for him. Anything.

And so here they were at an impasse. All he had to do was offer her what she wanted.

Great to help out a friend, but at the same time he was held back by…abject *fear*. Fear, that was it. The increased heart rate, sweaty palms, gut clench. He was scared as hell at the prospect of it all, of letting everyone down. Of not loving enough. Or, worse, loving too much. And he knew damned well how that panned out. He wouldn't be able to function around a child or be part of her cosy family. But if he didn't do it then she'd be forced to choose someone she didn't know or give up altogether—and he knew, too, that that was not part of her dream.

Despite all the late-night musings and the words going round and round in his head, he knew it was the most stupid idea he'd ever had.

But the words lingered. Lingered still as he saw her shrug her shoulders. As she turned her back to him and opened the car door. Lingered as he watched her swipe her hand across her face to stop a rogue tear. She wouldn't even allow herself to show her bitter disappointment. That almost broke him in two.

It would cost him little in time and effort. Not overtly anyway. He'd have to deal with the ramifications later. But right now his friend was hurting and there was something he could do to help. One singular thing. He could be that guy. The one he wanted to be, the one who took an emotional risk and helped a friend in need, whatever the personal cost.

Before he'd had a chance to second guess himself the words were tumbling out. 'Georgie, wait. I'll do it.'

Her voice was small and he could hear the pain, and yet deep down there was some hope as she turned to face him. 'Do what?'

'I'll be the donor.'

'You? *You?* Why?' Her laugh was bordering on sarcastic.

He took a step forward. 'Because I'm taking you seriously. This is what you want. What you deserve.'

She wagged her finger, fast. 'Oh, no. No. No. No. No. No. No. Not happening.'

'Unless you have a particular aversion to passing along my DNA? If I were to look objectively I'd say I was pretty okay. I'm a doctor, so not dumb. Oh, and my compassion knows no bounds. Apparently you like that in a father figure. I'm funny—always a winner.' He pointed to his abs, which he sucked in for effect. 'And pretty much the most devastatingly good-looking man in town.'

And bingo—his aid work meant he'd be out of the country for most of the rest of his life if he wanted. So he wouldn't be forced into any emotional attachment. This was a purely altruistic act. Which begged the question—what the hell did he want?

This wasn't about him, he reminded himself. It was about Georgie. 'How could you not want to use my *sperm*?' He whispered the last word as reality started to seep through his feel-good fuzzies.

The sarcasm melted away and the laugh was pure Georgie. 'Yeah, right. That's objective? Don't get above yourself. For one, you have a slightly crooked nose.'

He ran his down his ethmoid bone and he gave

her his profile view. 'Rugby injury, not genetic. Besides, you can hardly see it.'

She cocked her hip to one side as she perused him. 'You have particularly broad shoulders.'

'Great for tackling and giving great hugs.' And he should know. He'd done it often enough. Usually as he was patting women on the back and wishing them well. *It wasn't them, it was him.*

She frowned. 'But not great for wearing halter-neck tops.'

'Ah shucks, and now you've spoilt my dress plans for tomorrow.' Funny, but it felt strange, being analysed in such a way by a friend.

'On the other hand, you do have…long legs.' Her voice cracked a little as her gaze scanned his trousers. Her pupils did a funny widening thing. A flash of something—and then it was gone. Two red spots appeared on her cheeks. 'Ahem, big feet.'

'And we all know what that means.' He winked. 'Any boy would be happy with the MacAllister brand of DNA. If you bottled it you'd get a fortune.'

'Oh, yeah? No girl wants big feet. Bad for shoe buying.' She gave him a final once-over glance.

Then her voice softened. 'Really, it's a lovely offer and I'd be stupid not to take you up on it. But what about you? You don't want this. You really don't want this.'

'But you do, Georgie.' There was a long beat while he tried to put into words the weird feelings he was experiencing. He could give her the chance she wanted, on one condition. 'But we'll need a contract. I don't want any involvement.'

'Oh.' Giving the minutest shake of her head, she held her palm up. 'You'll be the baby daddy but don't want to be *the* daddy?'

'Yep.'

'Oh. Okay. Then I'm utterly shocked that you've offered. Why would you do that?'

Not wanting to dig up something he'd pushed to the darkest part of his soul, he gave her the scantest of explanations. 'Happy families isn't my style. But a happy Georgie is. I'll do it. Just agree before I change my mind.'

'Oh, this is fast and so out of left field.' She put a hand to his shoulder, ran her fingers down his arm. And in the cool late summer evening goosebumps followed the trail of her warm skin against his. 'Can I think about it? Get used to the idea?'

'Sure.' He needed time too, his chest felt blown wide open.

'It would mean a lot of changes. For us.'

'I know. I realise that.' And if it hadn't been Georgie's dream on the line, no way would he ever contemplate something like this.

She looked hesitant, shocked, but hopeful. 'So… well, we could have a contract similar to the clinic's standard donor document. We can use that as a blueprint. If that's what you really want?'

'That's what I want. No involvement, nothing.'

'I won't ask you for anything else. Ever. Trust me.'

He did. Absolutely. He just wasn't sure how much he could trust himself. 'Yes. Definitely. A contract will be best.'

'And it'll mean tests. Soon. Like this week.'

'Whatever it takes.' Although the altruistic vibe was fast morphing into panic.

'Oh, my God, is this really happening?' She reached round his waist and pulled him into one of her generous hugs. His nostrils filled with her perfume and he fought a sudden urge not to let go.

Her body felt good close to his. She was soft in his arms and her head against his chest made his heart hurt a little. He'd missed her these last few weeks. Especially these last few days. They never argued.

And this...was just a hug. Nothing strange there. She gave them all the time. And yet... He was aware of the softness of her body, the curve of her waist... He swallowed.

Nah. She felt just the same as always. Just the same old Georgie. She turned her head and looked up at him, her dark eyes dancing with excitement, the evening sun catching her profile. For a second she just looked into his eyes. One. Two. He lost count. She had amazing eyes. Flecked with warm gold and honey that matched her hair. His gaze drifted across the face he knew so well, and a shiver of something he didn't want to recognise tightened through him.

She pulled away quickly and the connection broke.

Thank God, because he was getting carried away in all her emotion. And that was definitely not something he was planning on doing. Emotional distance was the only thing that stopped him wreaking any more damage on those he loved. Hell, he was his father's son after all. Emotional distance was what MacAllister men did better than anyone else. But somehow he didn't think that that admission would go down well on Georgie's tick list.

'Thank you. Thank you so much. It means a lot to me.' She placed a gentle kiss on his cheek. Again with the goosebumps. This time they prickled all the way to his gut and lower. 'I'll mull it over and…um…let you know? Soon as possible?'

'Okay, and I'll get the turkey baster sorted for when you say yes.' Now he needed to ignore the strange feelings and off-load some of this ache in his chest. He saw a damned long run in his immediate future.

Her demeanour changed. She brushed a hand down over her scrub trousers, all business and organisation as she took a shaky little step away from him. 'Like I said, we'll do it the clinic way.'

'For sure. Any other way would be just too—'

Her head tilted a little to the side. 'Ick?'

He grinned. 'Is that a technical term?'

'Absolutely. For that weird feeling you get when you think about sleeping with your best friend? Like sex with your cousin? Right? Weird.' Shuddering, she looked to him for reassurance.

Which he gave unreservedly. 'Right. Yes. Ick's the word.'

The notion of them having sex had rarely arisen. Back in the early days he'd caught himself looking at her and wondering. She'd walked through his dreams many nights. He'd tried to imagine what kissing her would have been like. How she would taste. How she would feel underneath him. Around him. But he'd never put any of that into words for fear she'd run a mile. He'd never asked more from her than what they'd already had and, frankly, he'd believed that any kind of fling would inevitably ruin the great friendship they'd built up.

She was worth more to him than just sex. And seeing as that was the only thing he ever offered to women, he'd never wanted to risk doing something so pointlessly stupid and losing her.

Plus, while Georgie was funny and loyal, she'd never made a move or seemed interested in him in that way. They'd had an implicit agreement that anything of a sexual nature could never happen. So he'd sublimated those imaginings until he'd stopped having them. Had lost himself in other women.

Which made it all the more nonsensical that he'd

started noticing things again...like her smell, the colour of her hair, her eyes. Surely it could only mean some sort of nostalgia for the younger Georgie in his past when the present was shifting out of his control?

CHAPTER THREE

Eight months ago...

Hey, stranger. Thought you'd want to know that your genius sperm has done what it was designed to do...I'm pregnant!

Great news. Congratulations.

FINALLY, AN ANSWER. Biggest news she'd ever had and not one exclamation mark. Not one. No cheers or fanfares. No questions. Was he not just a little curious? Pleased for her? Maybe it was the whole emotionless text thing stuffing up the sentiment of his message, but hadn't the man heard about emoticons?

Disappointed, Georgie texted him back.

I'm so excited! :) Catch up soon?

Sure. Things are a bit busy right now. Packing. South Sudan. In two days. I'll try come over to say bye.

Okay, your call.

He was heading off again and he'd try to come and see her? *Try?* What the hell…? Packing didn't take two whole days. He was the world's lightest traveller.

And, actually, it was her call just as much as his. Worrying about contacting him had never been an issue before and it shouldn't be now just because she was carrying his baby. *No. Her* baby. He'd made that very clear. But surely they could still be friends? She wasn't going to allow this to change what they had. Why should pregnancy make a difference?

But it did, she realised. Not just to her relationship with Liam, but to her. She was going to be a mum. *A mother.* With a family. Something she'd never had before. She was going to be part of something…more.

She put a hand to her very flat, very *un*pregnant-looking stomach and her heart did another flip. It was still so early, too early to grow attached; any number of things could go wrong. But it was already too late. Her stomach tumbled as she closed her eyes, imagining.

Hey, there, little one. Nice to meet you.

And that was about all she dared say. She felt something tug deep inside her. These days she seemed to be so emotional about things. About the baby. About Liam…

Well, if he wasn't going to make an effort then she damn well would. She wanted to celebrate and send him off on his travels with no tension between them. Georgie stabbed his number into the phone and left a message: 'Hey, step away from your backpack. Let's do something. I won't take no for an answer. I get the feeling you're avoiding me. But if you are, please don't admit it. Just say you've been busy. Mission Bay? Six-thirty. I'm hiring bikes. No excuses.'

'Are you bonkers or just straight up certifiable?' Three hours later his voice, behind her, although irritated and loud, made her heart jig in her chest. He'd turned up at least, and for that she was grateful. 'Cycling? In your condition? Seriously?'

'Oh, for goodness' sake, I'm fine. How many times have we done this?' She turned and pretended to scowl, but her scowl dropped the moment she set eyes on him. He was wearing a scruffy old T-shirt that hugged his toned muscles and was the same vibrant blue as his eyes. Faded jeans graced his long legs, framing his bum…and, no, she'd never really studied it before, but it was deliciously gorgeous. No wonder he had a queue of women trying to encourage him to commit.

Heat hit her cheeks and shimmied down to her belly, where it transformed into *What would he be like in bed?*

And that was just one of too many thoughts about him recently that were way out of line.

To distract herself from staring too long at the man who had suddenly become a whole new fascination for her, she clipped on her helmet and prepared to use up some of this nervous energy. Pregnant, yes. Petrified, indeedy. Strangely excited just to see her long-lost best mate? Very definitely. And that made her legs twitch and her stomach roll.

'I needed some fresh air. It's such a beautiful evening and it's the weekend tomorrow. Freedom! We could get fish and chips and eat them on the beach later.'

He frowned and pointed to her helmet. 'Take it off, Georgie. It's too dangerous. We haven't been cycling for years, you could fall off. Why you suddenly want to do it now I don't know.'

'Because it used to be fun and I don't know why we got out of the habit of doing it. I want the fun back.' She shook her head in defiance. 'And stop being ridiculous. You're a doctor, you know very well that at this stage in pregnancy it's perfectly fine to exercise. Come on, I'll be fine, it's not as if I'm bungee jumping. Although, there is a free slot at the Skytower at eight. So if we hurry…' She handed him his helmet and stood, arms crossed over her chest, until he'd put it on over that grumpy face. 'Breathe, Liam. Breathe. It was a joke. And do try to keep up!'

The sea air was filled with salt and heat and the smell of a distant barbecue. Overhead, seagulls dived and squawked, making the most of a bright summer evening's scavenging. Mission Bay was, as always, filled with smiling people, cycling, blading or running along the seaside promenade. On the right, beyond small beach inlets and a turquoise sea dotted with anchored yachts, the mighty volcanic Rangitoto Island stood verdant and powerful. On the left they cycled past coastal suburbia, higgledy-piggledy candy-coloured houses clinging to the steep hillside.

Georgie pedalled hard, keeping him in her slipstream, ignoring his concerned cries. She could do this. She needed to do this to show him—and herself—that she was still the same old Georgie. And if she could also purge those weird fluttery feelings that seemed to happen whenever she saw him, that would be even better. Because this new Georgie who kept popping up with hot thoughts about Liam was unsettling in the extreme.

Usually he raced ahead, screaming over his shoulder for her to go faster, but today he seemed happy to pootle behind. She had the distinct feeling that, in his own way, he was keeping watch over her.

After a few kilometres, pedalling towards towering city skyscrapers, she turned and cycled back to the row of Victorian buildings flanking a children's playground and large fountain. Toddlers kicked and splashed in the spraying water, watched over by attentive parents.

Georgie braked, imagining being here some time in the future, showing her little one the exciting new world. Making everything a game, lining up her pram with the others, chatting to parents about nappy changing, bedtimes and the terrible twos. Her heart zinged. It seemed that, despite all her best efforts, she was starting to see everything through a different, pregnancy-coloured lens. With a heavy heart she glanced at the young dads splashing around and on the reserve, throwing balls to their sons, cheering, encouraging and, most of all, laughing.

Liam had been definite in his refusal to be a father. She understood that some people didn't have the need for kids in their lives, but that didn't mean she liked the idea. How could someone not want to know their own flesh and blood? It had been a question burning through her for her whole life. How could you just walk away and not want to be found, not want to make contact? What the hell ever happened to unconditional love?

It went against everything she knew about him. He was gregarious, funny, and cared deeply about the people he helped. But if he really meant he wasn't going to be involved she'd have to be Mum and Dad to her child. After all, in the children's home where she'd eventually settled, one parent was always better than none at all.

As Liam approached she flicked the bike into gear and cycled on to a small caravan advertising fish and chips and ice-cold drinks. 'Usual? Snapper?'

'Of course. And a large portion of chips. Tomato sauce...' He grinned, pointing to a can of cola. 'And all the trimmings.'

'I don't know where you put it all.' His belly was hard and taut. Body lean. Again with the full-on flush as she looked at him, this was becoming an uncomfortable habit. 'If I ate half of what you ate I'd be the side of a house.'

'You can't exactly worry about putting on weight now, can you?' He laughed and gave her a look she couldn't quite decipher.

Having returned their bikes to the hire shop, they walked in step down to the beach and found a spot on the sand in the warm, soothing last rays of the day. Liam sat beside her and they ate out of the paper in companionable silence, pausing every now and then to comment on the food. The fish was divine, as always, the chips hot and salty, the cola too cold and too fizzy. Everything seemed exactly the same as it always was, except that it wasn't. She didn't know how to begin to have any kind of conversation that referred to being pregnant without causing another rift between them.

In the end she decided that rather than going over and over things in her head she was just going to say what was bothering her. She waited until he met her eyes. 'I wanted to say thank you, thank you, thank you for what you did.'

'It's fine. Honestly. Congratulations. You must be pleased.' He didn't look fine, he looked troubled as he leaned in and kissed her cheek, long eyelashes grazing her skin. 'You're looking good. Feeling okay so far?'

'Feeling a little numb all round, to be honest. It's real and happening and I can't quite believe it. I'm so lucky for it to have worked first time round. But it does happen.' She ran her palm across her tender breasts. 'No morning sickness yet, but my boobs are pretty sore.'

'Yeah. It happens. Wait till the varicose veins and heartburn kick in then you'll really be rocking.' He gave her a small smile, smoothing the tiny lines around his eyes, and for a second she was ten years younger, meeting him for the first time. All über-confident medical student who had been knocked sideways by the tiniest of beings—so small she'd fitted almost into the palm of his hand. Never had Georgie seen anyone look so frightened by something so frail, the cheery self-assurance whipped from him as if he'd been sucker-punched.

He'd been honest and open and warm. And since then she'd stood with pride at his graduation, cheered him on the sidelines at rugby games, dragged him kicking and screaming to ballet performances and musical theatre, entirely happy with what he'd had to give her. Just a simple, uncomplicated friendship.

But now his eyes roved her face and then his gaze dipped to where her hand was over her breast. Suddenly she felt a little exposed and hot again under his scrutiny. She kept her eyes focused on the top of his head but eventually he looked back at her as if he was going to speak. A flash of something rippled through those ocean-blue eyes. Something that connected with her, something more than warm, which made her belly clutch and her cheeks burn. Heat prickled through her, intense and breath-sapping.

Her fingers ached to just reach out and touch his cheek. Just touch it. To see what his skin felt like.

To feel his breath on her face. Her mouth watered just looking at his lips. Open a little. Just a little... Her breath hitched. He was so close. His familiar scent of male and fresh air wrapped around her like a blanket.

Close enough to—

He shook his head as if confused and disorientated. Then he shifted away and focused on the remainder of his food. Meanwhile, she breathed out slowly, trying to steady her ridiculously sputtering heartbeat. Had she imagined that flash of heat? Those feelings?

Yes.

It was all just her stupid clunky imagination.

She would rather die than ask him and be laughed at...or worse. That kind of conversational subject was explicitly off limits and would only cause tension. It was bad enough that she'd created this difficult atmosphere in the first place. But now, to... Oh, my God. The thought flitted into her brain and rooted itself there, so obvious, so immense, so downright out of this world... *No.* Surely not. She didn't. Couldn't.

She fancied him? Fancied the pants off Liam MacAllister? The guy she'd got drunk with, thrown up on, told her deepest dirty secrets to? She wanted to kiss him? Really? Truly? Her heart thudded with a sinking realisation. Things between them were complicated enough, not least because he was going halfway across the world in less than twenty-four hours and she had no idea when she would see him next.

She couldn't want him, and he certainly wouldn't want her, especially with a baby in tow. Not now. Not ever. End of.

Hell, no.

Georgie was wearing a soft white lacy bra.

That was all Liam could think of. Not how amazing it was that she was pregnant. Although that was pretty amazing. Foolish and foolhardy and well beyond his comprehension too. But she did have a kind of warm glow about her, a softness he'd never seen before. He was no longer even registering how far beyond stupid she'd been to race along the pavement on two thin wheels when anything could have happened to her.

No, the only thing that took up room in his thick head was that her small perfect breasts were covered in lace.

As she leaned forward to take another hot chip, her top gaped a little more and he caught a glimpse of dark nipples. Cream skin. He swallowed. Dragged his gaze away and looked out at the boats bobbing on the turquoise water. What the hell was wrong with him?

Why, when he needed to put distance between them, had that whole concept suddenly become too hard to contemplate? He'd gone from not thinking about her in that way to not being able to stop thinking about her in the matter of a few weeks. He'd kept away, making excuses not to see her, just to get his head around everything. And it had failed spectacularly because the moment she'd told him she was getting on a saddle he'd thundered down here with a distinct determination to convince her not to. He'd always teased her, had fun with her, joked around with her, but never until now had he had this need to protect her. Even if it was from herself.

And he was damned sure it wasn't just because she was pregnant. But he wished to hell it was. Because that was none of his business. Because that he could distance himself from.

Couldn't he?

Man, his life was changing in a direction that was beyond his control and it was taking a lot of getting used to. His life, yes. But another life, a new life, was growing inside her and he was struggling to get past that.

After finishing her dinner and crinkling up the paper into a tight ball, she spoke. 'You didn't have to sneak into the clinic during my lunch hour, you know. I would have given you some space.'

'It just didn't feel right.' He looked everywhere but at her. The finer details of how he'd provided the sperm were definitely not for this conversation. Even more, he'd really not wanted to alert her to the fact he'd been in her workplace, doing the deed in a side room. 'Man, they ask a lot of questions.'

'Tell me about it. They always ask a heap of stuff about your parents too. Any genetic conditions, inherited diseases. Has either parent had cancer, heart problems, high blood pressure? It kills me just a little bit to not know. In some ways it's a whole clean slate and I don't know about any inherited illnesses that may be hanging over my head. But in other ways it's a jigsaw, trying to piece bits together.' She shrugged, trying for nonchalance, but Liam knew just how much she'd ached to know just something about her mum and dad. 'I don't even know who I got my eye colour from, for God's sake.'

He wanted to say it didn't matter. Because even if you did know who your parents were, it didn't mean a damned thing. It sure as hell didn't mean they loved you. Or maybe that was just his. But, then, how could he blame them? 'Well, at least you know little Nugget there will have big beautiful blue ones, to break the girls' hearts.'

'Or brown. She could have my brown ones.' She glanced over at him with a curious look and he immediately regretted mentioning any kind of pet name. He was not going to get involved. He would not feel anything for this baby. Which was currently only a collection of cells, not a baby at all. Not really.

His chest tightened. Who was he trying to fool? He could barely look at Georgie without imagining what was growing in her belly.

Who. Who was growing in her belly. *His baby.* He was going to be a father. And what had seemed such a simple warm-hearted gesture to help out a friend a few weeks ago had taken on a whole new meaning. This was real. This was happening. She was having his baby.

For a moment he allowed himself the luxury of the thrill of that prospect, let the overpowering innate need to protect overwhelm him.

Then he remembered a very long time ago, as a young boy of eight, the excitement deep in his heart as he'd felt a baby's kick. His hand on a swollen bump. The soft, cooing voice. A new life.

Then it was gone.

Ice-cold dread stole across him like a shadow. It didn't matter how far you ran, your nightmares still caught up with you.

He quickly tried to focus on something else. 'So, plans for the weekend? After the bungee is it whitewater rafting? Paragliding? How about base jumping? All perfectly suitable under the circumstances.'

'First I thought I'd go running with the bulls, then perhaps a little heli-skiing.' She threw the rolled-up paper ball at him. Missed. Completely. 'Idiot!'

He threw it back at her. 'Bingo. On the head. Your aim is appalling.'

'Show-off!' She threw it towards him. Missed

by a mile. Went to grab it. He reached it first and held it high above her head. Way out of her reach. She jumped to get it. Failed. Jumped again. Then she playfully poked him in the stomach so he flinched. 'Ouch!'

'Yes! Got it.'

He grabbed her arms and pulled her into a hug. Tickled her ribs until she yelped for mercy. Felt the soft heat of her breath on his skin. The way she moulded into him. Warm. 'Play fair.'

'Says the man with elastic arms. You have a natural advantage.'

'And you...'

Grinning and breathless, she pulled away, but not before he'd got a noseful of her flowery scent. She smelt like everything good. Everything fresh and vibrant and new. Something spiralled through him. A keening need. Rippling to his heart, where it wrapped itself into a ball of content, then lower to his groin, where content rapidly turned into a fiery need.

He let her go as his world shifted slightly. This could not be happening.

She sat back down, pink-cheeked but smiling. 'Actually, I thought I'd rip up the carpet in the spare room and see what's underneath. I'm hoping it's going to be one of those miracle moments— *Ooh, look, the last owner covered a perfectly intact parquet floor*—like on the DIY TV shows. But somehow I doubt it.'

'So do I. You'll be lucky if there's a decent layer of concrete there. Thinking about your dilapidated house makes me laugh. Either that or I'd cry. It needs serious work.' And thinking about something tangible and solid made a lot more sense than thinking about the searing lusty reaction he'd just had that had thrown him way off kilter. 'Don't get your hopes up. I've seen that old scabby carpet. The walls. The roof. My guess is that the previous owners only spent time covering up just how badly falling down the place was.'

'Aw, you know it was all I could afford. And it's a nice neighbourhood, good school zone, so will be worth a lot more by the time I've finished. Worst house on the best street and all that. And the roof is sound, it just needs some TLC.' She pouted a little and his gaze zeroed in on her mouth. Plump lips. Slightly parted. The tiniest glisten of moisture. He leaned over and dabbed a drop of ketchup away from her bottom lip. His thumb brushed against warmth. And his body overreacted again in some kind of total body heat swamp, accompanied by a strange tachycardia that knocked hard against his rib cage. The beach seemed to go fuzzy out of his peripheral vision as she blinked up at him, surprised by the sudden contact. Her lips parted a fraction more and if he leaned in he could have placed his over them.

And now he was seriously losing his mind.

Clearly he needed to get laid and quickly. With someone else.

Georgie moved away, frowning. She might have said his name. He didn't know. He willed his breathing back to normal.

Where were they? Oh, yes. The house. For God's sake, he needed to get up and go. This was crazy. This irrational pointless need thrumming through his veins. Crazy and sudden and he didn't know what the hell he was doing any more. Or where this had come from. But he wished it would go as suddenly as it arrived. 'It'll be great when you're done. Lots of potential.'

'So you said when I bought it. But now I've got to capitalise on that. I've chosen some paint. I thought a soft cream would be nice and I'll add colour with blinds and cushions, nursery furniture. I saw a great changing table in a second-hand shop down the road from work—all it needs is a lick of paint, I'm not going to be one of those mums who—'

'A bit early for nesting, surely?' He gathered all the wrappers up then stood, offering his hand to pull her up.

She threw him a look filled with hurt, brushed her clothes down and reached for her bag. 'Well, I've got to start somewhere. Nine months flies by, believe me. I see it all the time at work—people often don't even come up with a name in that time.'

Ignoring his hand, she stood without help and looked out at the ocean. Her shoulders taut, back rigid. Her jaw tightened.

He'd meant that she shouldn't be too sure that this early pregnancy would last the course, that she needed to wait before she spent money on things. Invested. But saying that would be crass. Distasteful. Working at the fertility clinic, she was well aware of all the pitfalls and rewards of pregnancy. And judging by the way her eyes glittered with any baby talk, she was very invested already.

When she turned back to him her eyes were blazing. 'You remember that first night in my house, Liam? When we sat on packing crates and talked all night about the plans I had for renovations?'

'Of course I do.'

'I'm still the same person. I still have that dream. It's going to be a fabulous place. Then I will sell it and climb that property ladder, baby in tow. We'll be zillionaires by the time I've finished. It just needs a bit of imagination, more time and a few willing hands.'

There was a long pause in which he felt sure she was waiting for him to offer to help with the decorating.

He'd returned from Pakistan planning on doing just that. But if he got involved in doing up her house that would mean more time spent with her and that was diametrically opposed to his plan. Which had been to ease himself out of her and her baby's lives. Gently. Without her really noticing. Just longer absences that she could fill with her antenatal classes, nursery shopping, other pregnant friends—because she must have them.

Everywhere he looked these days there were blossoming bellies and tiny squawking babies.

But now, seeing her pregnant and the immediate emotions that instilled in him, his plan seemed like a crock full of madness.

So all the more reason for him to get out quickly. He couldn't be ruled by emotions, he never let that happen in his professional or his personal life. It was too dangerous to do otherwise.

'Anyhoo...' Her eyes were clouded now as she blinked away. She rooted in her bag and pulled out a folder of papers, clearly trying to keep her voice steady. Goddamn, everything he did hurt her. She cleared her throat. 'Here's your signed copy of the contract from the clinic. Helen was supposed to mail it to you, but I offered to bring it along here instead. As you saw, it's pretty standard stuff. You get no claims, no guardianship or visitation rights, you're not a legal parent, you have no parental rights...yada-yada. Just what you wanted.'

'Oh. Okay. Great. Thanks.' In black and white it seemed so cold-hearted. And yet it absolved him of everything. No responsibilities. He took it and shoved it in to his backpack. He didn't need to reread it. He was signing every right to this child away.

Truth was, his thoughts about this baby were so blurred now. He'd thought it would be easy to walk away. But…well, it wasn't easy at all. He felt like he was giving his child the same fate he'd had—a life with little contact with his father. A life wanting something…guidance, truth, recognition. He couldn't give his child that. He just couldn't. But what could he give? What did he have left?

Georgie peered up at him and everything he knew about her was in that guarded look in her eyes. She understood his pain, but was equally angry. She was putting her needs first. And she needed to, he didn't blame her a jot for that. 'That's what you really want, isn't it, Liam? You don't want to help me get a nursery ready—that is clear. Or choose decor. Or talk about baby things. You don't want me to be pregnant. You don't want any of this…'

'Look, Geo, that's not it. I'm thrilled for you. I am. It's what you want and you look so happy, how could I not be pleased for you? I thought this was what you wanted.'

'Me too. But I don't know how you can do it. The more I think about it, the more I don't understand you. I've known all along that you cut yourself off from any kind of decent meaningful human connection…' She twisted in the sand and stepped towards him. 'So just explain to me one thing: what are you so afraid of?'

'I'm not afraid of anything.' And that was the biggest lie he'd ever told. He was afraid of the responsibility of another baby's life, of not being able to protect it from harm. Of loving too much. Of dealing with the utter heartbreak if something went wrong, because he didn't think he could live through that again. His heart raced as blood drained from his head, from his face. 'Nothing.'

'I watched you, Liam…that day in Resus, when your whole world crumbled at the sight of a sick baby. I know you are carrying some terrible burden and, through knowing you for ten years, I think it has something to do with your family. Your sister Lauren?'

He railed around, wishing he didn't know her so well, wishing she couldn't see through the barriers he'd erected. 'It has got nothing to do with anyone.'

'If you choose to let whatever happened colour everything you do for the rest of your life then I can't help you. And I want to, I really do. But I can't bear that every time I mention my baby— *our* baby—you flinch. So I'm going to do this my own way. I'm sorry if that doesn't work for you. Just go off to the South Sudan and do your precious job.'

'What?' His heart thumped harder, fast and furious. 'Is this about my job now as well? You don't like it that I'm going to be leaving all the time, is that it?'

'It's about everything, Liam. About your attitude, about your refusal to admit what's bothering you, the damned contract that means you will willingly let our friendship irrevocably change and allow a baby to be fatherless, and, yes, it's about your job. It's dangerous, and scary for those of us left behind.'

He shoved his hands in his pockets. He could barely look at her. By donating his...by delivering the goods, he'd done what he'd thought was the right thing—he *had* done the right thing—but the fallout kept coming. 'That job keeps me sane.'

'And drives me mad with worry. But I don't

know why we're even bothering talking about this. You've got your contract, you can go off unhindered by any kind of sense of responsibility.'

Responsibility? That was the one single thing that drove him to do what he did. Every damned day.

She whirled around and stalked away, but paused, momentarily to turn back. Scraping her hair back from her face, she glared at him, her body language so at odds with her words. 'Stay safe.'

CHAPTER FOUR

Four months ago...

'ONCE THE PAIN relief kicks in you can take him to X-Ray. Let's see exactly how far up the little tyke stuffed the ball bearing, shall we? Depending on where it is, he might need a sedative for us to get it out. But we need to know more before we do anything else.' Through the fog of his sleep-deprived brain Liam offered the concerned mum a smile. Just a little shut-eye between his plane hitting the tarmac and coming into work would have been nice. Still, boys would be boys, and stuffing things up nostrils was par for the course for a four-year-old.

Hopeful images of a little boy who looked a lot like him flashed through his head. He batted them away. He'd call Georgie and talk to her *later*, explain his plan, what he wanted...once he'd worked out exactly what it was he was going to say. Theoretically it made sense to have some contact with his baby. He'd be responsible for finances and guidance, provide things. No emotional involvement. No day-to-day stuff—he didn't want to tread on Georgie's toes. But enough that his child would be able to identify him as his father. He was responsible, for God's sake.

All very good in theory, but in practice he had no idea.

Maybe this was just another of his ludicrous plans that would be fraught with endless fallout. But somehow he did not like the idea of being a dad and not having at least some contact with the child.

The little boy's mum laughed, but Liam could see by her lined forehead and forced smile that she was still anxious. It didn't matter what befell a kid, their parent always worried.

'I don't know why he decided it needed to go all the way up his nose. I just wish he hadn't found it at all. I'll kill his dad when we get home. Leaving little things on the floor is so dangerous.'

'I guess having kids means big changes. It takes a bit of getting used to.'

That thought had been running over and over

in his head since he'd left. Would he be like that with his child? Worried sick if it stuffed something up its nose? Would he refuse to let them play outside in case they injured themselves? He'd seen extremes in this job. Neglect that almost tore his heart in two, and the worried well who caused a fuss over nothing. Where children were concerned, it was difficult to get the balance right. But generally it didn't matter where he was— flooded Pakistan, drought-ridden Africa—parents were the same the world over. They loved. They gave their children what they could. They worried.

He tried to find the wee lad a smile.

The boy grinned back. With sticky-out ears beneath sand-coloured hair he was pretty cute. And now, with the analgesic kicking in, clearly unbothered by the metal ball in his left nostril. 'I liked it. It was silver. I wanted to smell it.'

'Oh.' Kids said the strangest things. Stupefied by his inadequacy where children were concerned, Liam wondered whether you should talk to them like adults or use special kiddy words. He stuck to plain and simple. 'Metal ball bearings don't have a smell, buddy. Now, don't put anything else up your nose. Not even your finger. Off you go.' He turned to the mum and relaxed a little. It was far easier to talk to a grown-up. 'See you when you get back from X-Ray.'

The kid laughed at Liam's grumbling stomach, clearly unfazed by whichever way Liam spoke to him. 'What's that funny noise?'

'It's…er…' Not often he was lost for words. 'I'm hungry. My tummy's asking for lunch.'

'Metal balls don't smell and tummies don't talk.'

'No. Well, I don't suppose they do. But they growl, like mine, so go on and get your picture taken so we can see inside you. Skedaddle.'

And lunch was supposed to have been six hours ago. But since then he'd had a steady stream of minor emergencies on top of a few pretty major ones. Now, shift almost over, he could finally go home. Looking forward to getting something into his stomach that wasn't yet another Sudanese stew or tasteless plane mush, he strode across the ER floor, past the whiteboard. And stopped. Turned. Refocused on the names. *What the…?*

White noise filled his ears, his appetite replaced by an empty hole deep in his gut as he hot-footed it back to Minors and threw the cubicle curtain open. Sure enough, she was there, head in her hands, making soft snuffling noises.

'Georgie? What the hell—?' Four months he'd lain sweltering in a too-hot tent and she'd been tattooed onto the back of his eyelids as he'd gone to sleep, their last conversation going over and over in his head. Making things right hadn't seemed possible from the dodgy dirty-walled internet cafés he'd visited sporadically, so his emails had been short and perfunctory.

He'd spent weeks wondering what he'd say when he saw her in person, how he'd feel when he saw her carrying his baby. How he'd feel when he saw her, period. He hated it that she had put a line under their friendship, ending everything so abruptly. But none of that mattered now, none of it.

He tugged her into his arms, hauled her head against his chest and stroked her back. 'Hey, don't cry. It's okay. It's okay. Whatever's happened we'll fix it. It's okay.'

Firm hands pressed on his chest and gripped his shirt. Her voice was low but not upset. In fact... was she laughing? 'Oh, my God! Liam. You're back! When?'

He'd finally stopped shaking enough to concentrate. Goddamned ER doctor and he'd crumbled the second he'd seen her name. *Georgie. The baby.* He didn't know which thought had come first— one had been so quickly followed by the other. And if that wasn't the most bizarre sequence of mind mess he didn't know what was.

And now she was here, damaged somehow— because this was where damaged people came. And that was just the staff. Worst-case scenarios flitted through his doctor's brain, fuelled by his own awful experiences. 'Early this morning. I was going to call you once I'd had a sleep, but they needed me here urgently. I didn't even get the chance to go home. But what the hell—?'

'Don't get carried away. And, no, I'm not crying.'

'What happened? The baby?' He took a step back and surveyed her belly with quick observations. She had a rounded-out bump now, small and perfect, but the rest of her was thin. Too thin. Grimy, dusty. None of this added up. 'Is the baby okay?'

'Yes, everything's fine. Except...' She finally

let him go and moved her hand away from her face. 'I hurt my eye.'

Her right eye was weeping, closed and puffy. Her cheek was swollen. 'Whoa. Great job. What did you do?'

'I smashed a wall through and got dust or shards of chipboard or plaster or something in it. It hurts like hell.' She grimaced, swabbing at her damp face with a dusty fist.

Thank God she was okay. Thank God the baby was okay. Unfamiliar feelings sliced through him, accompanied by a strange lumpy sensation in his throat that made words hard to find. 'You were knocking a wall through? On your own? Are you mad?' He hauled in air. 'Don't answer that. I know the answer. Which one?'

'The kitchen-lounge one. I thought it'd be nice to have one big sunny room all finished in time for Christmas. Imagine what fun it'll be to have dinner in there.'

'The legendary Georgie Taylor Christmas, with enough liquor to sink a ship. And enough food to feed an army. But couldn't it have waited until you got help? Christmas is months away.'

'I've got to be prepared, Liam. This renovating

lark takes time and I want Christmas to be perfect this year. I have grand plans.' With her one good eye she glared at him. 'If all you're going to do is tell me off, I'll ask for someone else to deal with my injury.'

'Go right ahead, missy. I think you'll find I'm the most experienced doctor here but, please, feel free to find someone better. I'll take you on a tour if you like. See if any one takes your fancy.' He thumbed the teary trail across her cheek. As he touched her an immediate heat suffused his body. He took his hand away, shaken by such an intense response. 'Oh, sorry, I forgot, you can't see.'

'Excuse my bluntness, Dr Mac, but your bedside manner is slipping. You're supposed to be nice to people when they come and see you with an injury. Basic ER doctoring.' She stuck her tongue out and if she'd felt any electric surge at his touch she didn't show it. He'd thought he'd purged her from his heart, that if he'd worked harder, faster, later then he wouldn't care so much. *Feel* so much. Too bad it hadn't worked. He didn't want to feel anything at all.

'Looks like I suck at interpersonal skills.' He

picked up her chart and feigned calmness. 'That was meant to be an apology, by the way.'

'Must try harder. See me after class.' Her lips pressed together tightly. She took a breath and let it out slowly. She definitely looked thinner than the last time he'd seen her, cheeks a little more hollow. Her hair, T-shirt and jeans were covered in bits of wood chip and plaster, but her eyes…well, her good eye had darkened shadows round it. She gave him a reluctant smile that had him craving more. 'Oh, Liam, I've missed you. Missed this.'

Me too. 'Okay. So sit still and let me have a good look.' He tipped her chin towards him. And, yes, it would break every damned oath he'd ever made but, hell, if those lips weren't made for kissing. Which would be a pretty dumb move all round, because things would never be the same again. 'Trust me, I'm a doctor.'

She laughed. 'The old ones are the best. I bet you use that on all incapacitated women?'

'Only the bloody foolish ones who are hell-bent on being so independent they do themselves a mischief. You tried to knock down a wall on your own?' He focused on her eye, not her lips. Damaged or downright sexy. Either way his heart hurt.

'And who else could help me? I'm hardly going to pay someone.'

'You could have waited for me.'

'We both know that that wasn't an ideal option. I didn't know when you were coming back or if we were still friends. Are we?'

The heart hurt intensified. 'Come on, we'll always be friends, whatever happens. Now, let me look.'

'Okay. Give it your best shot.' She managed to open her eyelid a tad but blinked so rapidly he knew it was painful. It slammed closed again, tears rolling down her cheek.

He grabbed a tissue and wiped them away, unwilling to risk a skin-on-skin encounter again. 'Hey, it's okay. I forgive you.'

One eye widened in disbelief. 'What? You? Forgive me? But you were the one—'

'Seriously, no need to cry over me.'

Her lips pursed. Pouted. 'I'm not crying over you, matey. I just can't stop it watering.'

He looked away and began writing on her charts, mainly because it was far easier to do that than look at her. At least he didn't want to kiss the charts better. 'Well, whatever you've done, you've made an almighty mess in there. We're going to need to give you an eye bath to get the gunk out and then get an ophthalmic opinion.'

Her shrugging shoulders confirmed her agreement. 'So you'd better get it organised, then. You must be busy with more needy people than me. I don't mind seeing someone else. That would be if I could see at all.'

'Actually, I'm finishing my shift very shortly. I've got one patient to review then I'll sort out your referral while you have an eye bath. As soon as I'm done I'll wait with you.'

She shook her head. 'No need, honestly. If you don't want to.'

'Of course I want to.' He wasn't letting her go that easily. 'I know I made you angry and for that I'm sorry. I know I can be blunt and unthinking at times, but I realise there are two of us in this friendship...'

'Three now,' she hissed at him, rubbing her belly. His heart gave a little jerk. *His baby.* At once he felt proud and anxious. Excited and terrified.

Protective. Should he say something now?

No. She was damaged and he needed to deal

with that, get things on a firmer footing. And work out exactly what it was he wanted to say. What kind of involvement he wanted. He rubbed his hand across his forehead. 'Come out with me for dinner, like old times. We could do fish and chips with extra grease, your favourite. Or curry. Thai, Chinese?'

'Urgh. Please. Don't mention—' She held up her hand then covered her mouth. 'I should have… Oh. No.' She grabbed the back of her chair and stood. Swayed a little.

'Should have what?'

She murmured through her fingers, 'Eaten something. I'm sorry, I have to—'

Then she was ripping back the curtain and staggering across the corridor to the toilet, leaving grubby handprints along the wall. He was beside her in a millisecond. Maybe she'd hit her head too and forgotten to mention it? Concussion? 'What's wrong?'

'Morning sickness? *Morning?* Yeah, right. Liars. All-day sickness, more like. Switches on at the thought of food. Goes away when I eat. In all this excitement I forgot to eat.' She pushed him back away from the bathroom door. 'Wait. Please, wait here. Before I chuck on your shoes.'

And he got a distinct impression that she probably didn't care if she did. 'No, Georgie, you can't see a thing. I will not wait. I will stay here and make sure you're okay.'

'Go do your patient review. You're not the boss of me.'

'How old are you?' He'd spent ten years getting to know that no one could ever be the boss of Georgie. He could hardly leave her and go back to ball-bearing-in-nostril kid when she was like this. 'You infuriating woman—'

But he stopped arguing as she slammed the door open and crouched down while he held her hair back in a thick makeshift ponytail. Her body shook. He held her steady.

This was his fault. He'd allowed this to happen. He'd facilitated this. He ran his hands across her back, felt the knobbly bones of her spine through her loose-fitting T-shirt. Jeans hanging off her hips. She was definitely thinner. This pregnancy was taking a toll on her and she was so damned proud she would never think of mentioning it. She needed a good meal. To be looked after. Someone to take care of her while she grew her baby, instead of believing she could do it all on her own. 'Does this happen a lot?'

'Enough.' She rocked back on her heels and wiped her mouth with toilet tissue.

Putting his hands under her arms, he hauled her up, made sure she was steady on her feet, watched her wash her hands and splash her face, wincing as cold water hit her eye. 'You're losing weight.'

She looked at him in the bathroom mirror, dried her hands and threw the paper towel in the bin. Peered at her eye in the glass. The swelling had worsened. Her one good eye pierced him. 'So are you.'

'South Sudan can do that to a guy.'

'Don't tell me you gave half your food away again?'

'I can survive. They don't have enough. I had plenty even with half-rations.'

'So how was it?'

'Messy. Murky. Complicated.' Like the rest of his life. 'But I'm back here and I want to know about you. How long have you been vomiting and how many times?'

'Simmer down. A few times a day. Counting

wasn't helping. Let's just say, too much. It's perfectly normal. It's supposed to go once I hit the
second trimester, so it'll be gone any day now.
I'm fine.'

Fine? She was a mess. 'And in between the vomiting you're working full time and then taking out
your frustration on your house walls? When do
you rest?'

She threw him a smile that stopped way short
of her dark eyes. 'Well, you know what they say
about giving a job to a busy person. That's me! I
like being busy.'

'No, you don't, Georgie. You like getting drunk
in grungy bars playing loud eighties rock an-
thems, you like blobbing on the couch and watching reruns of your favourite soaps until you can
say the dialogue better than the actors, you like
strawberry ice cream, but not berry swirl. You
like doing nothing at all if you can help it. You
do not like to be busy.'

Uh-oh. Hip-planting was occurring. Both hands
fisted. Bad sign. 'Well, you can add doing renovations when pregnant to that list. Go figure, you
learn something new about people every day.'

'You know what they say about people like you?'

'No.' She turned to him and swayed a little, her cheeks drained of colour. Her eyes fluttered closed as she steadied herself, leaning against the sink, hands flopped to her sides. She looked exhausted. He wanted to swoop her into his arms, wrap her up in bed and look after her. As if she'd ever let him. 'Tell me, Liam, what do they say?'

'That only the pig-headed, wilful, independent and stubborn will not listen to anyone else. To the detriment of their health. You can't get sick, this baby needs you to be well. You need to stop and rest.' And he was not going to stand by and let anything bad happen. Period.

But contrary to everything he expected from her, she didn't rally. Her shoulders sagged as she gripped the sink, her voice so small he had to strain to hear her. 'Okay, okay, I get it. I'm done arguing. Whatever you say, you're the doc.'

Things must be bad. Never in all the years he'd known her had she so much as uttered a single word that would make her appear less than über-confident and capable.

He took her by the shoulders and steered her out into the waiting room. Found her a chair. Sat her in it. Put a finger over her mouth to hush any complaints.

She needed him and he wasn't going to let her get sick on his watch. It wasn't as if she could call a relative to come look after her—she didn't have any. No one to look out for her, to give her a break when she needed it. To take the baby for a few hours when she needed sleep. To babysit. Did she really have a clue how hard this parenting was going to be? 'You're going to start taking it easy. Doctor's orders.'

CHAPTER FIVE

'LET ME HELP YOU. Be careful, you have a nasty corneal abrasion.'

'So you keep saying. Urgh. So I'll play pirates and keep wearing the eye patch, me hearty.' Georgie had to confess that even though the thick white cotton wool patch didn't help much with healing, and made her look a lot like a numpty, it protected her eye from the glare of her house lights and made her think seriously about wearing safety goggles in the future.

But one thing she'd be reluctant to confess out loud was that the moment Liam had said she needed to take things easy it had felt as if a huge weight had been lifted from her shoulders. Because it was all very well trying to be big and brave and bold but sometimes, just sometimes, she tired of having to rely solely on herself for everything.

A deep breath escaped her lungs as Liam pushed

the front door open. She was home. She could relax. At least in theory. It was a little harder in practice, having him in her space, being big and bold for her. Why had he suddenly come over all macho? Why did that make him even more desirable?

For that matter, why hadn't her desire dampened down over the last few months? And why was a man in combat kit and biker boots infinitely more attractive than anything else? She turned on the doorstep. Pregnant and now injured, this was not a good time to be finding her friend attractive. 'Thanks for getting me home. I'll be fine from here. Maybe we could catch up tomorrow when we're both feeling better.'

'Hey, what's the hurry? Are you scared about what I'll do?' He shook his head, eyes glittering with tease as he surveyed her body. If she wasn't mistaken, tension of a very sexual kind rippled between them.

Air whooshed into her lungs as she gave a sharp intake of breath. She wasn't afraid of Liam at all, she was more scared about what *she* might do, suddenly alone with him and very, very hot. 'No... er...I—'

'Don't panic. If it's a total mess I won't get mad. I'm here to help.'

He was talking about the state of her house. Not...*of course not*...anything else. 'I'll be okay. Honestly. Go home, you look beat, Liam. You must be jet-lagged and knackered.'

'Listen to yourself, Geo. You're not letting me help. You don't have to do everything on your own.'

'Of course I do. And I like it. That way I don't have to compromise on anyone else's plans, don't have to work to their timetable, I can just please myself.' She placed her hand against the wall and kept him on the doorstep.

He shook his head. 'Has anyone ever told you that you're the most stubborn person in the world?'

'You? Many times. But you're saying it as if I might care. And I don't.'

'Well, today you're my responsibility and I promised the discharging medical officer I'd take care of you.'

'But you were the discharging medical officer.'

'Go figure. So I'll fix you some dinner, have a look at the damage you've inflicted on your poor house. Make sure you're OK. Then, once I'm satisfied, I'll leave.' He went to squeeze past her, but she blocked his way.

'Promise?'

He frowned. 'If that's what you want.'

She wanted him to be happy about the baby— the single most important thing, and which he'd hardly mentioned. That was all. Well, and to hold her again. Possibly kiss her. Make out, maybe… But that would be a wish too far. 'What do you want, Liam?'

'To make sure you're safe, crazy lady. That's all.'

As he peered through the dust and grime he scratched his head, fluffing his short dark hair into little tufts. 'Bloody hell, Georgie. It's worse than I imagined.' He stepped in, walked across the floor, leaving large thick footprints in the grey film that coated everything. 'What the hell have you done?'

She hid a smile as she followed him into the house where she'd half knocked through the wall, making her downstairs pretty much open-plan. She had grand plans for this room, plans she'd been aching to share with someone. Him, mainly.

And even though she'd been beyond angry with

him for the last couple of months, it was good to be able to see him—through her one useful eye—and talk to him. Because she'd been honest when she'd said she'd missed him.

She hadn't expected to have those strange feelings rattling through her again, though. She'd put it down to a cluster of hormones, but when he'd held her, cradling her head like she was something very precious, her heart had done a little leap. More, her body had started to hum with something dangerous. It was a bad idea, having him in her space. 'Personally, I think it's looking great. That old partition wall made everything dark and dingy. Just needs a little bit of cosmetic work and it'll be fine.'

'Plus finishing off. Cornices, a new floor.' He tapped along what remained of the plasterboard wall. 'You go and sit down in the lounge, if you can find the sofa under all this mess. I'll finish this off, clear up, then sort out something to eat.'

'You're hardly dressed for it.'

He looked down at his ex-army fatigues. 'They're old. I don't care. You just sit tight. That is, Miss Independent, if you know how to let someone else do the work.' He picked up the hammer and his forearms tightened. Capable hands, plus mussed-up hair already, and he hadn't even lifted a finger. How was she going to cope?

For a few minutes she lay back on her couch, closed her eyes and let relaxation take hold. It was lovely to lie there, listening to the crash of the hammer. The crumble of plaster, his deep male grunts as he swung and hit. He worked for a while then there was silence.

It stretched.

Suddenly interested in what was happening—or not—Georgie opened her eye and peered across the settling dust.

Oh, good Lord. Her stomach contracted as she inhaled a mouth full of dust. He'd taken off his shirt and was now measuring across the space with an industrial tape measure. Defined muscles stretched and contracted as he moved. Tight abs ridged down to his trouser waistband, a sexy smattering of dark hair pointed to a promised land. The man had no business looking like that, all sunburnt and muscular and just too damned hot. She swallowed, her mouth suddenly dry. Her throat was tight. Her breathing came quick and fast.

Staring was rude.

She reclosed her eye.

No good.

She wanted to look again. It was like watching bad reality TV: she knew she shouldn't watch, but she couldn't help herself. The man was gorgeous. And, heck, she'd always known what his body was like. Days spent with him at the beach had had little effect on her in the past. But now... Wow. He'd developed strength and solidity and muscles. Filled out into those broad shoulders. Her body hummed with need.

He turned to face her. 'You okay? You need anything?'

Not the kind of thing he'd want to give her. 'I'm just fine, thanks. But I wanted to let you know I'm sorry that you left and we'd fallen out. I was worried about you, you know, the whole time.'

He winked at her. 'Forgiven. Just about. I hate this arguing. It's not like us. We don't argue.'

So many firsts for them. 'You do realise that not once have you asked me for any details about the baby? About when it's due. Or if I've had any scans. Which I have.'

'I didn't know where to start.' Dropping the

hammer to the floor, he looked lost. Shame faced. Terrified. 'This is all so new. It's pretty intense to get my head round.'

He was a long way behind her in this. For the last few months she'd been wondering whether her child having a father around mattered. Whether, in the long term, it would matter to him.

God, there were so many things she hadn't thought of when she'd gone hurtling into this process. Things she should have talked to him about. Things that could make or break their friendship for ever. It was already spinning out of control.

She pulled a scrap of paper from her purse, taking another risk at rejection. If he baulked at this then she'd reconsider. She got up and walked over to him. 'Here, have a look. An early scan. More of a blob really, but there she is.'

'She?' He took the paper in a shaking hand but didn't look at it. His face paled, he swallowed. And again. 'Too early to talk about gender, isn't it?'

She shrugged. 'I just think of her as a girl. Don't know why.' She pushed the paper closer to him. 'Take a look.'

His fingers closed over the top corner of the

paper. He took a deep breath and looked down. No sound. No emotion. Nothing flickered across his face. Nothing to register that this was his child. That she was carrying his baby. Then he raised his head and gave her the scan picture back. 'My God.'

His voice was hollow and raw and she wondered what he was thinking. Maybe he was happy that she was happy but didn't know how to show it.

Her throat filled. 'I don't know what to say or do to make this easier…or less complicated. I know this is going to sound very selfish, but I want everything, Liam. I want this baby, but I don't want to lose your friendship.'

'And I…'

She thought he was going to say more but he didn't. His hands dropped to his sides as he shook his head and turned away.

Despite his doubts, he'd given her this gift. How could she have been so angry with him? He looked so empty and confused that she stepped forward and wrapped her arms round him, pulled him to her, and he responded by holding her close.

Her hands ran over muscles, dips and grooves of naked hot skin, slick with a light sheen of sweat.

Her heart began to pound as awareness surged through her. His smell of surgical soap, aftershave and pure male heat filled the air. She inhaled it. And again.

His face was inches from hers. His breath feathered her skin. But she daren't move. Something stirred inside her deep and low. Her breasts tingled for his touch. Was he feeling this too? She hoped…but then what? This whole crazy messed-up situation didn't need complicating further. If he knew what was running through her brain right this second he'd probably walk away and never come back. For all she knew, he was probably planning that anyway.

Keeping her eyes tightly closed, she held her breath, felt him relax against her, felt his grip on her lessen. She didn't want him to let go. She wanted…

'Thanks for that, you old bat,' he whispered, lips pressed against her cheek, his scent intensified along with the tingling through her body, pooling in her groin. She couldn't think of anything but him, being in his arms, how good this felt.

Heat swamped her. There was no point pretending that what she felt for him wasn't real, that this was just a hormonal response. For goodness' sake, she'd been struggling with these weird emotions for months now. And, yes, she wanted to kiss him. She had to know what he tasted like. How he would feel.

With every risk of him leaving—and with no thought for the consequences—she turned her head, met his mouth. Felt his surprise resonate against her lips. Then a groan. A growl. A need.

Liam registered the first touch of Georgie's lips as his heart slammed loud and thunderous in his chest. For one split second a dark corner some-where in his brain considered that this was the far side of madness—but then that thought was gone and he was left with nothing but heat and need raging through his veins.

Cupping her face in his hands, he opened his mouth to her. Felt her shaking body, heard the gut-tural moan from her throat, felt her tight fists grip his trouser waistband as he dragged her closer. And each of her responses fed his need. She tasted wet and hot and soft. Of salty tears and fresh pure joy. He closed his eyes at the sweet sensations she instilled in him.

Her hands made a slow trail to his backside as she clamped her body to his and she moaned again as she felt him harden at the press of her hips. He liked the way she felt against him. Liked the feel of her fingers on his body. The thrill of her touch.

As his hands slid down her back he brushed against her bra strap and the memory of those perfect nipples covered in lace made him ache to touch them. Slipping his hand under her T-shirt, he worked his fingers to her breast, felt the hardening nipples beneath silk. He wanted to feel them against his skin. Naked. Wanted to suck those dark buds into his mouth. To taste her everywhere. Wanted to feel her around him.

'Oh, God, Liam.'

'Georgie…' He opened his eyes, and immediately registered the harsh reality. *Damn.* This was Georgie. She was injured and pregnant and he was supposed to be looking after her.

Not taking advantage of her. This was Georgie. His best friend. The hands-off friend.

Who was pregnant.

With his child.

And, yes—ever since he'd held that picture in his hand and felt the deep singular ache in his heart he'd known that he'd fight heaven and earth for his baby. This was something that was a part of him and he couldn't turn his back on that.

He'd been about to tell her his plan. About the financial help he'd decided he wanted to give. About giving his son or daughter the best. Because they deserved it, Georgie did too. But… when it had come to it, after holding the scan in his hands, he'd panicked. He needed to be sure.

And then…this…had blown his heart wide open.

My God. Kissing Georgie.

In the cold stark light of day that dark corner of doubt started to flourish. Another person he would let down. His life was littered them. He sure as hell didn't want to include Georgie and the baby in that line-up.

The shock of what they were doing made him break away. He did it with little finesse and immediately saw the embarrassment or disappointment or just plain confusion flash across her gaze.

What the hell just happened? He coughed, cleared his throat, tried to sound a lot less shaken up than he felt. 'Well, that was unexpected. And not at all like kissing my cousin. But, then, Mike never was much good at tongues, apparently. You, however…'

'Always the joker.' She twisted away and stalked back into the lounge area, wringing her hands in front of her, clearly trying to work out how they'd gone from friends to…this. And what the heck they were supposed to do now they'd crossed an unspoken line. 'I'm sorry. I shouldn't have done that.'

'No.' He followed her but couldn't find it in him to sit down. His first and only instinct was to get the hell out. But running out on a woman who was sick and confused would make him a jerk and a coward. Although he couldn't help feeling that he'd already started to put distance there. He wasn't sitting down and talking reasonably, he was edging subconsciously closer to the door. He made himself stand still and focused on her. '*We* shouldn't have done that.'

'No, Liam. *I* kissed you. Embarrassment totally one hundred per cent complete.'

And he'd kissed her back—without any encouragement. What happened to reining in his libido, like any other decent man would? But something a lot like a mind meld had happened, pushing him to continue, and he'd been unable to stop.

Her lips were a little swollen, her good eye misty, hair messy, as if she'd just scrambled out of bed. She looked sexier than anyone he'd ever seen. Sexy and very off limits.

Actually, sexy, off limits and torn. 'Really, Liam, I think you should go.'

'Yes. I'll come back and finish this off another time.' He went to get his T-shirt, shook off some of the debris stuck to it before pulling it over his head. 'I should order you a pizza or something. You need to eat. Regularly and properly.'

'I can manage a phone quite well.' Waving her hand in front of her, she gave him a brief smile that was laced with hurt. 'Please, just go. You're officially off the hook. Go, and let me die a thousand embarrassed deaths in peace.'

He didn't know what was running through her mind, but he'd take a big guess that it wasn't him actually agreeing with her and leaving. The last thing she needed right now was uncertainty. But everything was messed up and muddied; there he was tangling her pregnancy with his feelings. He was having a hard time separating the baby issue from his attraction to Georgie. If they didn't get everything out in the open, this would be hanging over them for ever. 'But shouldn't we talk about what just happened?'

'No. That's not going to get us anywhere but deeper in trouble. It's pretty clear from your face that you're shocked. Please. Please. Just go.'

'I'll be back tomorrow to help you.'

'Off the hook, I said. I can manage. Please...' She was biting her bottom lip and looking so regretful that he did her bidding. She didn't want him around. And the truth was he didn't much feel like staying when his head and his body were so much at odds and he was at risk of making things worse. Or, even more catastrophic in the long run, helping to make her feel better in the only way he wanted to right now, which would be a one-way ticket to the far side of stupid.

CHAPTER SIX

MORTIFIED. JUST DOWNRIGHT mortified. Georgie
was surprised her cheeks hadn't burnt a hole right
through her pillow. Twelve hours later and she was
still…utterly mortified. Half peering, half feeling
her way around her house, she went downstairs to
the kitchen, finished wet dusting all the surfaces,
popped the kettle on and contemplated pushing
two pieces of wholegrain bread into the toaster.
Then gave up on the idea. Ruining friendships
had sent her appetite running and hiding along
with her pride.

And, okay, so he'd kissed her back, and appeared to have been enjoying it, but the moment
he'd cut loose and let her go she'd seen doubt and
fear and confusion run across those eyes. Eyes
that had turned, once again, a darker shade of
navy.

But, man, he'd tasted so good. *Felt* so good.
Until the moment he'd jerked away and she'd

wished she could have been swallowed up in the house's perennial dust cloud and whirled back to five minutes previously. Before the kiss that had probably, finally, broken their friendship.

And it was all her fault. She'd pushed him in one direction to give her his sperm, acknowledged he didn't want to go there at all but had done it anyway, and then had pulled him to her in a selfish moment of unwarranted and uninhibited need. Putting her head in her hands, she leaned against the grey kitchen bench, dusty again already, and groaned. Stupid. *Stupid.*

God knew where they'd go from here.

The doorbell rang quick and sharp and then Liam was calling out, and then standing in her lounge, muscled arms filled with brushes and buckets and tools, which he put on the floor in the corner of the room.

'Morning.' He stopped short and frowned, and her stomach contracted. 'Holy cow, you look awful.'

'Thanks a bunch. So do you. Why don't you come right in and make yourself at home?' She tried to make her voice sound nonchalant instead of shaky, but it all just came out weird and high-pitched. She was a little bit relieved to see that he looked like he'd just finished night duty—tired, paler and shadowed with a perfectly stubbled jaw. Which inevitably made her stomach contract again, but this time for a totally different reason.

She peered up at him, trying to measure his mood while at the same time trying to quell the nausea in the pit of her stomach. And she knew it was nothing to do with her morning sickness and everything to do with kissing her oldest mate— and even now, despite the mortification, wanting to do it again. The hot spots on her cheeks reappeared. 'I thought I said you didn't have to come and help. I know you have little time off as it is without bothering about me. I can manage fine.'

'And leave you here knowing what disaster was lurking behind this door? No way. No doubt if I left you in here with a hammer for any length of time you'd be completely blind and crippled within the hour. So basically I'm doing my colleagues at A and E a favour by keeping you out of their hair.' He made no effort to hide his smile. 'I thought we should go out for a while first, take a walk to the French market. Get out of this dust bowl and clear your lungs.' AKA not wanting to be in a confined space with her. She understood, loud and clear. 'You don't need an asthma attack added to your medical history.'

'My lungs are perfectly clear, thank you.' *Unlike my head*, she thought, which was filled with grimy confusion. 'The dust settles downwards all over the surfaces rather than floating upwards to my bedroom.' And at the mere mention of where she slept, usually near-naked, she had an unwelcome image of him also naked, in her sheets. Okay, so not unwelcome…in fact, very welcome indeed. Just unrealistic. And never going to happen. 'So…er…how are you? Good sleep?'

And maybe it was the mention of her bed that did funny things to him too, because all of a sudden his bravado slipped, he shoved his hands deep in his pockets and his gaze was not at her, but beyond, or around, or anywhere else but meeting her eyes. *Eye.*

An awkward unspoken tension hovered between them as he shifted from one foot to the other. 'I'm fine. How are you feeling? How's the eye? Using the drops as prescribed?'

'Yes, Dr MacAllister.' She patted the new patch gently, knowing that, added to the sleepless eye

bags and the uncombed hair, it gave her a patheti-
cally ill look. Still, having managed perfectly well
for twenty-eight years pretty much on her own,
she was far from fragile, but it did feel nice to
have someone ask how she was feeling, even if it
was just to avoid talking about the kiss or what
the heck they should do now. 'The prickly head-
ache's gone. I feel okay, a little sore, but raring to
get going in here.'

'Well, first brioche and espresso are calling.
Then you can go and do whatever you want to do
for the day and leave me in peace to get this place
sorted. I've got more stuff in the car—plaster, roll-
ers, cornices, skirting, protective goggles and face
masks. It'll keep me busy for a few…' His fingers
speared his hair as he looked at the room, the
magnitude of the utter mess they'd made clearly
dawning. *And not just the house.* She'd made a
mess of everything. 'Weeks.'

And he was also playing the *let's not talk about
it* game. She could do that too. And perhaps,
by the time they'd got to the market normality
would be restored and her appetite would come
out of hiding. 'Okay. Well, I'll just drag a brush

through my hair and grab a jumper. Give me a minute or two.'

The sky was a brilliant cloudless cobalt blue as they strode down the hill, past rows of perfectly maintained colonial-style houses, just like hers was going to be…possibly next millennium. Luckily the market wasn't far so they didn't have too many moments of difficult silence to fill before they got there.

They walked through the car park to the stalls dotted around the forecourt of a large open-fronted building selling everything French. Colourful Provençale earthenware sat next to tins of *foie gras* and jars of bright thick jams; soft linens and dainty sprigs of lavender graced traditional wooden dressers; blue and white chequered tablecloths covered a hotchpotch of mismatched tables. People sat around, chatting and eating and laughing.

A stack of antique furniture sat in one corner of the building, rickety tables and chairs, kitchen and bedroom heirloom pieces. Georgie spied a quaint rocking bassinet in need of a little care and attention, adorned with the softest cream-coloured blankets and the cutest coverlets, and her heart did a little jig. It was perfect. But, as with most things here, it was also too far out of her price bracket.

She sighed, dragging herself away from such beautiful things. Buying would have to happen when she could afford it, not when it took her fancy. Liam noticed her gaze drift back to the bassinet but, then, he would. Annoyingly, he knew her through and through. Her heart jig went into a serious funeral dirge. It seemed everything was an issue between them these days. He nodded at the bassinet. 'Planning ahead?'

'Window shopping. At least that's free. I have to get my priorities straight. Firstly, I have to provide a decent place to sleep. Then I have to provide something to sleep in.'

'Babies cost a lot, eh? So much to think about, it's mind-blowing.' His forehead crinkled as he frowned. He looked as if he was about to say something, then changed his mind and tugged her to the juice bar instead. 'Okay, now you're going to have a fresh juice. Then we'll get a decent coffee and something to eat.'

'But—'

He placed a gentle palm against the small of her back and manoeuvred her towards the juice stall.

'No buts. And we're going to be the same as we always are when we come here. We're going to *ooh* at the cheese and hold our noses at the smell. And buy way too much and not eat it all. And then we'll have to fumigate your kitchen-diner-lounge room thing, whatever you want to call it.'

'I call it my living area, and it's going to be fabulous. But unfortunately I'm not going to eat any unprocessed soft cheese there or anywhere else. Along with alcohol, pâté and most kinds of processed meat that I love, stinky cheese is out for a while. Remember?' She patted her stomach. Damn the man, she was going to mention her pregnancy. It was part of her. Soon it would be most of her, plumping her out like a huge fat cushion. And then there'd be no denying it. Whether he liked it or not.

To her surprise, he grinned.

'Okay, so you're going to look at the cheese section and be downright miserable. Walk straight past the pâté, giving it a cold hard stare. Cast eye-daggers on that devilish salami and *jambon*. And then order a double helping of *pain au chocolat* and a *chocolat chaud* with lashings of cream, and still wallow in what you can't have instead of what you've got. Which, in my book, is three helpings of chocolate and it's not even ten o'clock.'

He stopped at the juice stall and ordered a freshly squeezed OJ for himself and a 'Brain Booster' for her, like always.

'Which is why you need this vitamin blast to counteract the sugar rush. And now we're going to talk about what happened last night, and when we've stopped cringing we're going to laugh about it. We will laugh. Eventually.'

At her shocked face he smiled again, but this time it was softer and more tender. And she liked it that he was trying to make things normal, that he was making sure she had the right things to eat, and that she was as content as she could be under the circumstances. This was the Liam she'd grown to love. Whoa. *Love?*

Platonically, yes. She loved him as any friend would love a friend. And fancied him, just a little bit. Which was understandable, because a lot of women did. He was just the type that appealed— dashing doctor with a great sense of humour and nice hands. Looking lower, she admired other parts of him too.

Okay, if he kept on staring at her and smiling like that she could definitely fancy him a lot.

'Na-ah.' Georgie shook her head as her cheeks heated again. 'I'm not going to talk about it, I'm just pretending it didn't happen.'

'Well, I'm not. That's not going to work. It's going to be the big elephant in the...market, stomping around with us for ever. So we'll acknowledge that it happened. We'll agree it was—'

'A mistake,' she butted in, before he could say anything else. Because that's what it had been. A huge silly mistake.

'Here you go, you two. Your usual. Beautiful day...' The juice lady passed over large plastic cups of vividly coloured juice with perfect timing. Georgie took hers and handed Liam his. Then she wandered through the stalls, perusing the locally grown fruit and vegetables, the huge bowls of oily olives and myriad savoury dips, and feigned interest in everything apart from this conversation.

He was by her side in a moment. On any other day she wouldn't have paid much attention but today all her body seemed interested in was getting closer to that smell, in being near him, in having his lips on her skin again. His mouth was dangerously close to her ear. 'I was going to say it was nice. More than nice. In fact, it was a bloody revelation. I didn't think you'd be so...unleashed. But if you want to say it was a mistake, go ahead.'

She twisted to see him, his eyes glinting with tease. And heat. 'It was a mistake. And I'm so-o-o embarrassed.'

His arm snaked across her shoulder and he wrapped her in a sort of guy-style headlock hug thing. Which shouldn't have been remotely sexy but was the biggest turn on since her lips had touched his last night. 'It's okay, Geo. We can move on. It is possible.'

'You think?' Wiggling from his grip, she faced him. 'I kissed you! In fact, I almost attacked you!' The clatter of teacups reverberated around the space, and then ended in an abrupt silence. People stared and then turned away and pretended not to stare, which made everything ten times worse. She lowered her voice and her words came out a lot like a hiss. 'But, then, you kiss so many women you probably didn't even think much about it.'

Hadn't he? Had it been really not special? Had she not turned him on while she'd been burning up? By saying they could move on, was he trying to say that he didn't want her? Which was what she wanted, wasn't it? An end to these weird feelings? So why did she feel as if she'd been stabbed through the gut?

'To be honest, it's all I've been thinking about for the last twelve hours.' He steered her to a table and sat her down, grinning. He was enjoying this. Well, of course he was, this was Liam, the great non-committer. 'But what I need to know, Geo, is why?'

'Well…' If she knew that, she'd be up for a Nobel prize or something. The secrets of the universe. The chemistry of attraction. The laws of inconvenience and mortification. All started and ended with the *but why?* of that kiss. 'Haven't you ever wondered about…you know…us? What it would be like? What we would be like?'

He shrugged his gorgeous shoulders, but a tiny muscle moved in his jaw. 'I seem to remember you used the descriptor *ick* the last time we talked about this. So, honestly, it wasn't something I imagined could happen. Then, suddenly…*wham.*'

'I attacked you. I did—*do*—think it's an ick idea. But, then, for some reason last night I felt really connected to you. I'm sorry.'

'Stop apologising. Never apologise for kissing like that.' The waitress brought their order and he took a bite from his *croque monsieur*, which oozed melted cheese over the plate and looked almost as delicious as the man sinking his teeth into it. He swallowed and took a sip of espresso. 'Do you think it's because of the baby? Is this all because I'm the father? Because, frankly, you never gave me any reason to think you liked me... in that way. And, yes, we're going to keep talking about it like we talk about everything, so take your hands away from your face.'

'No. Yes. No. I don't know. It's all become too complicated. I felt weird when I saw you that day in the bar after you came back from Pakistan. Something was different. You seemed different, I felt different. Maybe it was the fertility drugs.' But that was a lame excuse. Lots of women took them and didn't go around kissing inappropriately. She finally had the courage to look up at him. Yes, something was still very definitely different. The feeling hadn't gone, it had got worse. 'Anyhoo, I got it out of my system last night, and we both know that nothing can happen, don't we...?'

'Absolutely. Understood.'

What she wanted him to say she didn't know. Except, possibly, that he wanted to do it again and again. That he fancied her in just the same way. Okay, she wanted the whole dang fairytale—but Liam had never been much of a Prince Charming, and she definitely didn't suit the Cinderella role, apart from the having no money bit. In that part she was absolutely typecast.

Placing his cup slowly into the white bone china saucer, Liam looked like he was carefully choosing the right words. 'We are in no state to start anything. Imagine if we did the sex thing and then fell out. Imagine if we took anything any further. Me the playboy and you pregnant and vulnerable. You need to think of the baby.'

'So I don't get to have a sex life? Women can have sex when they're pregnant. Numpty.' Her eyes almost pinging out of her head, she picked up her fork and pointed it at him. 'And I am not vulnerable. Dare to say that again and I'll fork you to death.'

'No, never. Please. Anything but that.' His voice rose a teasing octave. Then got serious. 'You are one of the strongest people I've met. It was the wrong choice of words. Your situation makes you vulnerable. But you need someone who'll stick around. Someone who—'

'Wants me?' She closed her eyes wishing to hell she hadn't said that. It sounded so needy, and she wasn't. Just uncertain. And frustrated. Because she wanted to kiss him, she wanted to take him to her bed and tangle in the sheets, like she'd imagined. She wanted him…in a way she hadn't known could be possible. But he didn't want her. And he was trying so hard to put it gently and nicely and in a friendly way. It was humiliating that he even thought she needed the gentle treatment.

A sharp twist of pain radiated through her solar plexus. Even her own mother hadn't wanted her and had left her in a box on steps outside a church hall with nothing except a small cream woollen blanket and the clothes she'd been wearing. No one had ever claimed her. And bureaucracy and mixed-up paperwork had meant she hadn't been put up for adoption until she'd been too old, so she'd never belonged. Period. No one had ever wanted her.

And to a certain extent Liam was right. He didn't stick around anywhere for long, his job took him to some of the most dangerous parts of the world, and for the most part she thought it was exciting, glamorous even. But in reality it was dangerous. He ran a serious risk of being killed, caught or tortured. Did she want that kind of anxiety to infiltrate her life and that of her child's from here on?

His warm hand covered hers. 'You know I wouldn't do anything to hurt you, right? But we can't put our whole friendship under threat because of curiosity. Things would inevitably change. They couldn't not change. Everything would come under the spotlight—past partners, broken promises, how we fill the dishwasher, whose turn it is to empty the bins. And everything we've ever done with other people will come under scrutiny too, what we've said, what we've done. There'll be expectations, and I'm not good with that. You know that. I don't want things to get complicated.'

Too late, mate. 'Like me having your baby?'

'Yeah. That. It's complicated already, without getting things involved sexually too. Not that I don't want to…wouldn't…you know…mind. That kiss wasn't ick. It was good. Very good.' He shook his head. 'God, this is awful. I think I preferred your way of pretending it didn't happen. Let's go back an hour, shall we?'

Or twelve?

He held her gaze for a few seconds and smiled apologetically. Then his smile melted. As if distracted by something over his shoulder, he turned away. When he looked back he didn't give her eye contact at all. Just stared down at his cup. 'And...'

'And?'

His head jerked up, and he looked spooked and shocked. 'Nothing. Forget it. Just that. I can't give you what you need.'

'I don't need anything. It was only a kiss.' But the caution in his eyes told her he had been about to say something else. Had broken off before he'd dared say it. What the hell? Her heart began to rattle against her rib cage. 'Wait a minute. What are you hiding?'

'Nothing. I don't know what you mean.'

'You look edgy and worried and I've seen that look on your face many times. Right before you give your poor sap of a girlfriend the old heave-ho.'

He looked down at his hands and dragged in a

breath. 'Georgie, there's something else. Something I've been meaning to say since I got back, but haven't…quite found the right words.'

The chocolate croissant felt like a hard lump in her churning stomach. Things had become really messed up. 'I won't jump you again, if that's what you're worried about.'

'Of course I'm not worried.' No? Well, he just looked it, then. 'I'm going to help you renovate your house, I promised I'd do that. And I will.'

She knew a man was stalling when she saw it. 'And then, when you've done your dutiful bit and fulfilled the promises, you're going to adhere to the baby daddy contract and do a runner.'

'Far from it. In fact, just the opposite.' He stood up, took her by the arm and began to walk back through the market. 'Not at all. Georgie, I know it's taken me a long time to outright say it, but I wanted to make sure. I was trying not to mess you around.'

'What? What is it?' *You've met someone. Someone important.* Words clogged in her throat, thick and fast. 'Spit it out, man. I'm on tenterhooks here.'

He gave her a sideways smile. 'Thing is, I do

want to be the father of this child. I want to pro-vide, I want to take responsibility for my baby.'

'What? *Your* baby? Your baby? Whoa. That's a surprise.'

'Yes. My baby. It's got my DNA. Just like we agreed. Like you wanted.'

'But you said…' All her ideas tumbled around in her head with a sharp mix of frustration.

All she'd known about him for ten years sug-gested he didn't want a child. He didn't want a family. He'd signed a damned contract, made that the only condition. So instead of being the far side of elated, her gut felt churned up. Would he change his mind again?

And again?

And then there was the small matter of the kiss, which coloured everything.

His involvement was what she'd wanted ever since he'd offered to be the donor, but this was not how she'd imagined it would make her feel.

Irritated, she shook her arm free from his. Shop-pers jostled against them as they headed back to-wards the house. The busy street was so not the place to be having this conversation. 'I know it's what I wanted, but I thought you didn't…weren't…

aren't…' She pulled herself together and chose bluntness and honesty. 'Why now? Why this all of a sudden? How can I trust that you'll take this seriously? You're so confusing.'

Unlike her, he seemed far from irritated, his voice steady and determined. 'It's not confusing at all. This is the most serious and the most single-minded I've ever been about anything.'

'And you decide to tell me now? Here, on Parnell Road?'

'Okay, I have to admit my timing's lousy.'

'You can say that again.' She whirled round to face him, her head woozy at the sudden and fundamental change in her life. She didn't know how she felt about this. He hadn't exactly declared his overwhelming love for the baby, and she didn't know how she *felt* about him—except that he'd just completely blindsided her and everything was getting more complicated by the second.

And more, she had to be sure this wasn't some passing phase he'd move out of next week, next month, next year. 'Is this some kind of misdirected duty thing? Because you don't get to do that. You don't get to mess around with other people's lives just because it makes you feel better. Here one minute, changing your mind the next.'

'I won't change my mind.'

She tried to stay calm. 'A contract has been signed, Liam. You're legally bound, remember? Clause number six? *"You will have no paternal rights whatsoever over the child, and will have no authority of any kind with respect to the child, or any decisions regarding the child."'*

'Whoa. Really? Off by heart?' He stared at her open-mouthed.

'What? I counsel about this exact dilemma every damned day, Liam. So I know the wording. Okay?'

'So you'll remember clause ten, then? You can agree to me having social contact—at your discretion.'

He'd certainly read it. He'd taken the time and effort to read and research. He was serious. 'Yes, I can, if I think contact will be good for the child. But what do you know about bringing up a child? About being a father? What's changed for you?'

Love, she thought. She hoped.

Because love for her child, even though it was

still so small and so precious, had changed her fundamentally.

But Liam's expression turned thunderous. 'This is ridiculous. I don't want to mess anyone around, I want to be involved—the two things are completely different. I knew you were going to react like this. You just don't want anyone butting in on your little family of two.'

'How dare you? I would love my baby to have a father, you know that. You know I want that more than anything.' She shook her head. Amazing that he could think that. 'Is that what you think of me? That I'm selfish? That I want to keep this child purely for myself, like some kind of...toy?'

'Of course not. But surely, as the father, I have a say in things?' He really meant it. He wanted to be part of this. But could she trust him to be wholly there for them?

'No. Actually, you don't. You signed your rights away. All I know is that not many months ago you demanded a contract and now you don't want that. Maybe next month you'll want the contract again.'

He stopped short, breathing hard, dragged a wad of paper out of his jacket pocket. 'Here. Here's the contract.' He held the papers up and tore them in half. Then half again. Then again. Pieces of ripped paper fluttered to her feet like large bits of confetti. Only this was the severing of something, not celebrating the uniting of something. 'I want to be a father. The father of the child you are carrying. My child.'

And the word 'love' is still not there.

She'd listened hard and it was still missing. No matter how much she wanted it to be there, no matter how much she strained to hear it in the cadence of his words, in the silence between them.

He wanted to be a father, but he didn't want to be a daddy. That was the fundamental difference. He wanted the label but not the emotional involvement. That was Liam through and through.

But, on the other hand, if he was truly serious and did want to be invoived, she couldn't deny him that, couldn't deny her child the right to know its father.

Why did this have to be so complicated? Why couldn't he have kept to his side of the deal? Why did she have to have developed more than friendly feelings for him? Those emotions were tainting things, making her think in a way she'd never done before. This whole morning wasn't about the kiss at all. It had never been about the kiss.

His hand was on her arm now. 'Georgie, I don't want to have this conversation here on the street and I don't want to argue. This was the furthest thing from my mind. You look upset and that really wasn't my intention. I honestly thought you'd be pleased.'

Pleased? If his intentions were genuine then she'd be delighted. How could she not want him to be a father? He was smart, funny and, if she was honest, would make a great daddy—if he stuck around long enough. And there it was again, her immediate concern: he just wasn't the staying sort of guy. For whatever reason—and she only knew half of his story—he didn't commit.

She picked the pieces of paper up and shoved them at him. Then hesitated on her doorstep. 'Can we talk later? This is pretty big for me, I need some time to think things through.'

'Yes, by all means, think it through.' He followed her up the steps and when it was clear he wasn't giving up, she took her key out of her bag. As he watched her he shook his head. 'But I need to say this now, Geo, and I need you to listen. It's tough work, bringing up a child. I don't want you to go through it on your own and I don't want our child to miss out on having a father. I know how that feels and I couldn't condemn my own flesh and blood to that kind of life. Don't you want me to be involved?'

'This is my flesh and blood too. My only flesh and blood. So I've got to be careful, make the right decisions.' At least he had a family. He might not want to have them, but he was tied to them. And now she would be tied to him for ever. Oh, why the hell hadn't she thought this through more thoroughly at the beginning? 'What exactly do you mean by "involved"? Cash? Because that's not enough. Is that why you're here? To pay us off or something?'

'It's been in my head for the last few weeks, I just didn't know how to say it. When to say it. What to say, even. But the more I see you, the more I think about it, the more it makes sense.'

'It's not about making sense, it's about how you feel. In here.' She touched her chest. It felt a little cracked open and raw. 'In your heart and your soul. You can't do something because it makes sense, otherwise we'd never do any of the rash, amazing stuff we do. Like this pregnancy thing from the start. None of it made sense, not to you or anyone else. But it did to me.'

'And it does to me now.'

His words hovered in the air as she thrust the key in the lock and threw the door open. She took several long deep breaths and tried to clear her thoughts.

Then tried to explain them to him. 'If I was going to co-parent I would expect a fully one hundred per cent committed father who was around, who wouldn't flinch during the darker times. Because there will be some, I'm sure.' And although she adored Liam, he wasn't reliable. He was away a lot of the time, never knowing when he'd be home. And she couldn't get past the fact that he'd told her that this baby plan was the worst thing he'd ever heard.

'It's got to be for ever, you can't change your mind again. I don't want to open our child up to a whole world of hurt. I saw plenty of kids at the home whose families made promises and broke them, and in the end broke their kids' hearts and crushed their spirits.'

'I know you had a hard time, Georgie. And

that's why I'm here now. So our child doesn't have to go through what you went through.'

'You have no idea. You don't know what it means to be alone. To make up a pretend family because you don't have any. To watch others being chosen. To wish that someone, anyone, would choose you. And to try to be, oh, so brave when they didn't, when inside every part of you is crumbling.' She would never crumble again. This child inside her gave her twice the strength and three times the resolve. 'This is your last chance to decide, Liam. I'll hold you to whatever decision you make now. This is it. No going back. No coming to me in three years, six, twelve and saying you made a mistake and you've changed your mind again. You have to be in or out—for ever.'

This was something Liam could answer. Because this was the one thing he knew. He would not let his child down. He'd known that with every damned fibre of his being since the moment he'd seen her carrying his child. Since he'd seen that scan of a real living being. His child. Their child.

Every single mention of a baby, every thought

of who was growing inside her, brought back the crushing pain again. And with that hurt still beating against his rib cage he knew he'd make every effort to make his child safe. Because that was his job. A father did that.

But he was also going to keep any emotions out of it. Because, hell, he needed to keep his heart safe, too. He would provide from a distance. He would have visits but he wouldn't—couldn't—put any of them at risk by allowing himself to care for them. He would treat his child with the same compassion and consideration he treated his patients, no more and certainly no less.

'I know what I said. I didn't think it through. But this is my child and my responsibility and I will never shirk from that. I don't want your experiences for our child, or mine either. This child will know he's always wanted.' This was not how Liam had imagined this scenario playing out, but he had to go with it. He'd already stumbled too far along without saying what he felt. Although he'd been shocked by the ferocity of Georgie's reaction. He'd seriously misjudged her. She was growing braver and stronger and more independent every moment she carried that baby. 'I am in it for ever.'

'How can I be sure?' Her hands were on her hips while her dark eyes blazed.

'So tearing up the contract isn't enough for you?'

'No. Actions speak, Liam. I want actions— and not dramatic hollow ones like those shreds of paper.'

Now this was well and truly out in the open he knew there could never be any more kisses. He needed to keep a good long distance from her, too. Anything else would make things far too complicated. They could both be good parents if they were a team, a *platonic* team. Messing with that, opening a whole potential for destruction, would be a recipe for disaster.

He knew how much pain a child suffered when their parents couldn't bear to look at each other. Knew how destructive it was, watching arguments unfold, always calculating when the bomb was going to drop. Always being on guard. Always feeling, believing, *knowing* that every single ounce of friction was his fault. He couldn't put his own child through that, so if there was no intimacy there would be no chance of that damaging scenario happening. 'You'll know, Georgie, because I'll damned well prove it to you.'

CHAPTER SEVEN

Three months ago...

'IT'LL KEEP ME *busy for weeks.*'

Ha. He wished.

By Liam's reckoning it should have been finished months ago, but whenever he turned around
this tinpot wreck of a house threw another job
at him. Georgie had been wrong about the roof.
With the winter came high winds that blew off
and cracked more than enough tiles for the whole
thing to need replacing.

Then there was the floor in the kitchen. Weath-
ered and abused over seventy years, it took four
consecutive weekends to sand it down enough
that it was even and usable. Then three coats of
varnish. A perfect parquet floor it was not, but it
was now an acceptably usable one. All done on
a tight budget, and fitted in between exhausting
twelve-hour shifts at work. It had taken a lot of
coercing Georgie to even allow him to do that.

Climbing down the stepladder from where he'd been fixing the new light fitting in the flash living area, he huffed out a long breath. He had to admit she'd had a point about knocking the wall down, the open-plan space was amazing. With the renovated floor and antique white walls it was impressively large and light, with a good flow from one area to the next. She'd managed to find, on the cheap from a trading website, a set of elegant French doors that opened the kitchen out onto the small deck. Beyond that was a riotous garden, overgrown and dingy. But he had no doubt she had plans for there too. The woman clearly had a gift for renovation.

A loud bang and a very unladylike curse came from above him. Liam was up the stairs and in the bathroom in two seconds flat. 'You okay? What the hell was that?'

'Just a little contretemps with a tin of paint. And...damn, I was so nearly finished.' From her crouched position on the floor she grimaced up at him as a pool of off-white gloop seeped across stained dustsheets. A paintbrush stuck out of her denim dungarees pockets, her face was splattered with paint and she wore a plastic carrier bag tied round her hair. She dabbed at the ever-increasing seepage with a rag, huffing and puffing a little. 'I'm going to have to nip out to the hardware store and get some more paint now. Do we need anything else?'

His eyes flickered from her to the stepladder, back to her. *Unbelievable.* 'You were painting the ceiling?'

'Um…yes?'

'After I specifically told you it was next on my list of jobs?'

'Um…yes.' This time there was no hint of apology. 'It needed doing and it was next on *my* list. I was free to do it, so I made a start.'

'Why can't you accept more than the slightest bit of help without a row? You are slowly driving me crazy. No—make that rapidly driving me crazy.' There was only so much independence a guy could take before it became downright stubbornness, and then it made him really mad. 'You were supposed to be taking a break.'

'Breaks are boring. There's nothing more satisfying than seeing the instant difference a coat of paint can make to a room. Look, isn't it great?'

She gestured at the white over the dirty green and, yes, it looked good. That was not the point.

'And risk a broken collarbone…or worse?' He didn't allow his brain to follow that train of thought. Already she was showing signs of discomfort with her growing bump—all it had needed was one wrong step. 'These ladders are unsteady, and those trainers have a slippery grip. You said so yourself.'

'I was fine.'

'Oh, clearly. So fine that you dropped the paint can?'

'No one likes a smartass.' With an irritated groan she whipped the plastic bag from her head and stuffed it into her pocket, then gripped the side of the bath to assist her to transition from sitting to standing—flatly refusing his outstretched hand. Once up she rubbed her back, which pushed out her stomach, fat and round and very obviously pregnant. Her face had filled out a little too, her long hair, which she'd piled on the top of her head in some sort of fancy clip, was glossy. Man, was it shiny, and it took him all his strength not to pull her close and inhale. Somehow the more annoying she became, the more he wanted her. Seemed he was hard-wired to protect her too.

But he'd never contemplated giving her this job and hadn't thought she'd be so hell-bent on doing what she wanted. How much did he need to do to show her he was invested too? She'd taken him at his word and had never referred to the contract again, but he knew she watched him and wondered. Every day. And every day he tried to prove to her he was up to the father job.

He just hadn't contemplated how hard it would be to keep his emotions out of the agenda.

'How about you sort out the cupboards in the kitchen instead, like we talked about earlier? I'll do this when I've finished the lights downstairs.'

And, yes, it was like this every week. She had a problem or, more usually, the house had a problem and he had an insatiable, irrational need to fix it. Except the biggest problem was that he shouldn't be here at all. The baby wasn't due for months, so in theory he could let her get on with it. But, well, he couldn't.

Her voice had a sudden edge to it. 'You can't bear to be in the same room as me for five minutes, can you?'

'Sorry? What on earth are you on about?'

'It's just that every time I go into a room you leave it. It's been going on for weeks, it's like there's a revolving door. Me. You. Me. You. I'm getting dizzy.'

'Ridiculous.' Truth was, he couldn't bear to *not* be in the same room. Being with her was killing him. A long, drawn-out agonising death of lust. He was doing this for the sake of his child, making sure they had everything they needed. At least, that was what he told himself, and not because he didn't want to wake up every morning and not have the prospect of seeing Georgie's smiling face or inhaling her scent that pervaded everything in the house.

'Is it me? Is it seeing me like this that you don't like?' She paraded in front of him, laughing, sticking her tummy out—there was a bubble where her belly button protruded. 'Because I happen to love it.'

He laughed. 'Or maybe it's a coincidence, ever thought of that? Perhaps I just always happen to be about to leave when you come dashing in. Bad timing, maybe, and you're looking for it so you have confirmation bias?'

'Yeah, right. Never try arguing with a know-it-all doctor. I notice it because it happens, matey. And don't deny it.'

Avoiding the wet paint, he took her hands and faced her, putting a serious tone in his voice, ignoring the immediate sharp jolt of electricity that ran through him as he touched her. 'Okay, yes, Geo, you're right. I'm sorry to have to break it to you, but you do look terrible, hideous, unsightly. In fact, I was going to ask you to cover up with that dust sheet. But now you've spilled on it I'll just have to put up with you as you are.' He laughed at her tongue sticking out of her mouth. 'Yeah, really, I can't bear being with you, and that's why I spend every spare hour here, doing your bidding.'

If only she knew how partly true those words were. It was seeing her, full stop. Seeing Georgie carrying his child, seeing her turn this dilapidated wreck into a home for her family. His family.

Every time he turned around there was something else: the piles of gifted baby clothes; the stockpile of nappies for newborns. The baby scans on the fridge—the most recent one at twenty weeks, where he could see every finger and toe.

Where the ribs encased his baby's fast-beating heart. Its chubby belly. The MacAllister nose.

Liam's heart swelled, then tightened. The memories threatened to swamp him again. He rubbed his chest, but the pain wasn't physical, it was psychological. And every time he saw Georgie it got worse.

And still he kept on coming back. Because he couldn't not. Because he couldn't contemplate an hour of his life when he didn't see her.

She dropped her hand from his grip and began wiping a paintbrush on the rim of the can. 'I am grateful, really. You don't have to give up all your spare time…' Her hand went to her belly and she made a sharp noise. 'Oh!'

He knew that look. He knew most of them now, thank God, because she never complained about any of the changes she was experiencing and he knew a few of them must have taken some getting used to. A rise of eyebrows and a gentle smile meant baby movement. A frown but determined-not-to-show-it stubbornly stiff jaw meant she had backache. A fist against her chest meant heartburn. He'd never been so aware of anyone in his whole life. 'Kicking again?'

'Yes. It doesn't hurt, it just makes me jump. It's weird. though, I don't know if I'll ever get used to it—it's like a whole crowd of butterflies stretching their wings. He's a little wriggler, this fella. I think he might be a martial arts expert when he grows up.'

He nodded towards her belly, his heart suddenly aching. 'She might be a dancer? Cheerleading? Gymnast? Scottish country dancing? That has kicks, doesn't it?'

Her eyebrows rose. 'The ones I learnt at school had a lot of skipping in circles and peeling off. I don't remember kicking. Apart from hot sharp prods to my nine-year-old partner's ankles. He had no clue what he was doing and was far happier pulling faces at his friends than swinging me in a do-si-do.'

Then clearly the boy had been a prize idiot.

Clearing the paint pot and mess out of the way, Liam stood her in front of him. Goddamn, she was beautiful, all flushed and smiling. He had to admit that being pregnant suited her. She'd never seemed so content. Apart from the odd moment when he'd catch her staring out of the window into the distance, or looking at him with a strange expression on her face. 'Show me?'

'What? Scottish dancing, in a tiny bathroom? Are you nuts? Silly me, of course you are.'

'Probably.' He took her hands in his and twirled her round. 'Like this?'

'Not even remotely.' Her head tipped back as she laughed, and for the first time in for ever things were back to normal between them. There was no baby, no contract, no tension, just two old friends messing about, like they'd done hundreds of times before. He twirled her again, faster, and caught her in his arms and she squealed, 'Stop! I'm covered in paint, my hands—'

'Are fine. Now, show me what to do. Like this?' He made a woeful attempt at a highland jig that had him stumbling over the stepladder. 'Clearly this needs practice.'

'And a lot more space.' She sucked in air, and again, doubling over with laughter. 'You are a lot worse than David Sterling.'

'David?'

'My nine-year-old partner. Broke my poor innocent heart when he kissed Amy Jenkins at the Year Four social, but at least he had rhythm.'

'I have rhythm.' And Georgie's heart was too damned precious to be broken again. Although Liam had a feeling that when all this was done, he'd be no better than David-bloody-Sterling.

'Oh, yeah?' She prodded him in the stomach, and he wondered whether that was a step up or down from being kicked in the ankle. 'I've seen your rhythm, mate, at Indigo, late at night, when you're filled with booze.'

'Bad, huh?'

'Actually, no, not at all. You're a good dancer, probably better than I am if I'm honest. But I'm not exactly going to want to admit that, am I?'

'You, my lady, are such a tease.' Feeling suddenly way out of his depth, he gave her a smile and it was pure stubborn willpower that stopped him from kissing her again.

'Really? You think so? I haven't even started.' She smiled back and the air between them stilled. Her hand slipped into his and squeezed, and she peered up at him through thick dark eyelashes. And he was sure she was just being Georgie, but that kiss hovered between them again, in her words, in the frisson of electricity that shivered through him. In the touch of skin on skin.

Her voice was raspy. 'Is it just me or is it very hot in here?'

'Hmm. You want to try peeling off? That might help. I could give you a hand. That is one thing I am very good at.' He rested his palm on her shoulder, toying with her T-shirt sleeve. Her pupils widened at his touch, heat misted her gaze and he knew then that she was struggling too. That just maybe she wanted the physical contact that he craved.

But, goddamn, he knew that was the most stupid thing to say, especially when they'd agreed to go back to situation normal between them— but it was out there now. He was tired of fighting this…and absolutely sure he shouldn't have said those words.

Time seemed to stretch and he didn't know what to do. Apologise? 'Georgie—'

'Oh. There it is again. It always takes me by surprise.' Shaking her hand free from his, she pressed her hand to her belly again watching his reaction, eyes wary now. She gave her head a little shake as she stepped away. 'And don't look so worried. I won't ask.'

'No.' She wasn't talking about his faux pas.

Once she'd asked him if she wanted to feel the baby kick and he'd refused. Point blank. And she'd never asked him again, but sometimes made a point of telling him when it was happening. And, by God, he wanted to, but he knew he couldn't, that with one touch of her, and of their baby, he'd be compelled to want more. And that didn't fit in with the emotionless parenting idea. Or the platonic parenting either.

The atmosphere in this minuscule room was reaching suffocation point, he needed to cut loose. 'Okay, so break time. You go put your feet up and I'll pop out to the hardware store. We need more sandpaper anyway. I'll get more paint, and I've got to get the right bulb for the light fitting—you got screw-in instead of bayonet.'

'Oops. Sorry. And when you come back, do you think we could spend more than two minutes in the same place? You won't run out on me?'

The ten-million-dollar question. 'This house is throwing us so many problems we have to divide and rule if we're going to win. Now, get that kettle on and I'll bring back biscuits for afternoon tea.'

'Are you sure?'

'Buying biscuits isn't exactly a difficult task. Of course I'm sure.' And, yes, he knew that wasn't what she'd meant. Dodging bullets seemed the aim of today. 'Chocolate? I know, white chocolate with raspberry. Two packets.'

She threw him a huge grin. 'Oh, Liam, I do like it when you talk dirty.'

He could have been out for another few months and it wouldn't have been enough to stop the need surging through his veins. In less than an hour he was back, trying to locate her, with his peace offering of her favourite biscuits. She wasn't in the kitchen, and the contents of the cupboards were still in boxes in the same place on the floor.

Wondering if she was actually doing as he'd suggested and taking a nap, or on that damned stepladder again, he mounted the stairs two by two, in total silence, glad that he'd fixed the creaking floorboards. The bathroom was empty.

Intrigued, he walked along to her bedroom, heard the radio, a song he didn't recognise, and she was singing along. It sounded ditsy and bright and he knew he should call out, make her aware of his presence, but something compelled him to be quiet as he approached her room. He told himself that he didn't want to make her jump.

She was standing in front of her closet, holding a black lace dress up against her body and looking in the mirror, turning from side to side, stretching the fabric across her belly. The work dungarees had gone, and now she was wearing flannel shorts and a baggy blue T-shirt. After a few seconds she frowned and threw the dress on the chair then shook her hair free from the hair slide. It cascaded down her back, a river of lush honey curls. Her breasts strained against the T-shirt. She was dusty and paint-streaked and fertile and ripe. She looked sexier than any skinny model on the front of the magazines, sexier than any woman he'd ever laid his eyes on. His heart stuttered. He took a step forward, paused.

She still hadn't heard him. Her humming continued. Taking a brush from the closet, she gathered a fistful of hair and started to brush rhythmically. And even though he knew he shouldn't be standing here, watching her do this, knew he was breaking a zillion unspoken promises they'd made in the aftermath of the single kiss, he still couldn't bring himself to speak. His throat was scratchy and raw, and his body was on fire. Each swipe through her hair was considered and resolute, her slender arm moving up and down, almost trance-like, what he could see of her face was calm and relaxed.

She was lost in thought, and still singing the up-beat, happy song. The reverence with which she took each brushstroke made his heart contract. The glossy sheen of her hair, the ridges of her back as she moved and shifted from foot to foot. Her body swayed a little, her backside bopping to and fro; and maybe it was the heat from before, the soft light in the room, the smell of her, the intimate nature of watching her, but he struggled with a powerful urge to carry her to her bed and make love to her.

He realised he was hard, that his hands were clenched against his body's strain towards her. That he had to consciously control his feet and make them still.

How could someone doing something as mundane as brushing their hair bring him to the edge of reason?

After a few moments she started to coil her hair back up onto the top of her head again—and that was it—his control was lost. In a second he was behind her, hands on hers, whispering close to her ear. 'Don't. Leave it down.'

In response to his sudden arrival she turned, shaking. Confusion racing across her face. And heat too. 'Oh, my God, Liam. You made me jump.'

'Sorry. I just…' He curled a lock of her hair around his fingers, pressed it to his mouth.

She placed her hands on his chest, that intimate gesture firing more need through him. 'What?'

'I can't do this any more.'

'Can't do what?'

'I can't keep away from you. Ever since that kiss I've been hiding out.'

She let out a long breath and her face creased into a soft smile. 'I knew it. I knew you were up to something. See. I told you. You are avoiding me. I was right. I'm always right.'

'Intuitive, perhaps. Give a guy a break. I was doing the right thing.' He touched her lips with the pad of his thumb, tracing the soft path, the delicate curve. They were pink and moist and kissable. He remembered how good she had tasted and suddenly he couldn't wait any longer. Finesse lost, he dragged her to him. 'Come here.'

She inhaled a stuttered breath, her lips opening a little, her body trembling. And made a concentrated effort to calm it. She briefly closed her eyes, opened them again. 'But I thought—'

'Shh… Thinking is overrated.' He reached his arms round her thickened waist, pulled her closer, spiked his hands through her hair and nuzzled right into it. Cupping the back of her head, he held her face close against his throat. Just held her against him until the shaking stopped. Until he could look at her again. He wanted to kiss her, but he wouldn't, wouldn't make things difficult. But he could hold her. Could feel her soft curves and taut belly pressing against him.

Breathe.

He prayed for the awareness and attraction to go, to be left here with just his old friend Georgie and nothing else, nothing complicated, because he knew that by taking those steps across the room he'd made things muddier than ever. But it was so compelling to hold her, to feel part of something so good. To be, for once in his life, actively looking forward, instead of just running from the past. To be accepted for the man he'd grown into.

Only now he knew how it felt, he didn't want to go back. Couldn't go back.

And then…the strangest of sensations. A tiny shiver against his hip, something almost ethereal…then it was gone.

His baby kicking.

Breathe.

But there was no oxygen. His chest hurt as he tried sucking in air, there was no space for anything more, emotion had filled his chest. A hard core of deep affection, a protective need, a desperate ache. And pride. His baby was moving, stirring in her belly. The shaking started again, but this time it was his body that was on the edge of control. 'Was that…?'

'The Scottish country dancer?' She pulled away a little and pressed a palm against his cheek. 'Yes, Liam. It was. There it is again.' She reached for his hand and pressed it against her bump. It was a flutter, not a whack. At least, not against his palm. The whack to his heart was mighty, though. And, God, no, he didn't want to feel this. Not this ache. Not this wanting. He didn't want to feel anything.

'Wow.' It was all he could manage. His throat was thick, his heart rampaging as all the pain came hurtling back. Pain, and yet something else, something profound that made his soul soar.

He didn't know what to think or what to say as he stepped back. He'd been trying to avoid any kind of physical contact with Georgie but he'd been unable to stay away, had been compelled to hold her. Now his reasoning had been proved right. All his emotions were getting tangled up and he didn't want that. Didn't want any emotions to get in the way of clear thinking.

Obviously sensing him detaching already, she tugged at his hand and pulled him to sit on the bed, her other hand stroking his shoulder. And it was tempting to sit with her and let her stroke the tensions away, but he couldn't sit, so instead he walked to the window and looked out at the encroaching night. Dark shadows filled the garden, like the dark shadows in his heart. He needed to find some place where he could breathe normally again.

Georgie's voice reached to him. 'I know this is hard for you. I just don't know why. I'm trying to understand, I really am, and I'm trying not to push, but I want to know. I might be able to help. Tell me about your sister, about...Lauren.'

'I can't…I don't want to.' Didn't want to spoil this moment, where *this* child was vivid and vibrant and had so much potential.

There was a long silence where the night breathed darkness into the room, and he thought she might have fallen asleep.

When she eventually spoke she sounded disappointed, and that was so not his intention. 'Some time, then. Tell me some time.'

But it was too much to ask of him. He didn't even know what words to use. Lauren…had been there, and then she hadn't been. And a huge hole had blown open in his eight-year-old heart that had never been filled with anything other than anger. At himself, mainly. At his parents.

And now… 'It'll only spoil everything.' He forced air out and inhaled again, trying to make some space in his chest, but still he felt constricted and tight. 'Let's get the hell out of here. I need to breathe.'

CHAPTER EIGHT

'THE PUDDING PLACE?'

'The right choice?'

'Oh, yes. Most definitely. These desserts are to die for. I couldn't think of anywhere more perfect.' Georgie's gaze slid over the rows and rows of chocolate éclairs, mini-Pavlovas and baked cheesecakes in the little dessert-only café, and then landed on Liam. She regarded him with caution. Whatever had been haunting him had passed. The shadows on his face had cleared a little, leaving him pale and reserved and yet trying so hard to act normal. She hadn't realised how emotionally distant he could make himself, even when he was in the same room.

For so many years his background had never mattered to her and she'd respected his need for privacy and put his quirky way with relationships down to immaturity at first, then pickiness, but now she believed it was meshed in fear. Of what, she wasn't sure. But now…now it meant everything. It meant the difference between them surviving this strange set-up they'd created or failing it.

If she could understand why he held back so much, perhaps she could help him surmount it. Because although he'd shown commitment with his time, she still didn't wholly trust that he would be there when it mattered. That he wouldn't change his mind and run. And she wasn't prepared to take that risk with her heart or her child's.

A waitress arrived and asked for their order. Georgie couldn't decide. 'I think I'll have one of each. To start with.'

'You sure that's enough?' Liam laughed, a little more carefree. 'Or are you just keeping it light until your appetite really gets going?'

'This eating-for-two business is pretty damned good. I'm going to miss it after the baby comes.'

He gave his order then turned the menu over and over in his hands as he spoke. 'In South Sudan it's not uncommon for women to have large families, sometimes up to twelve kids. Imagine the fun you'd have then: eating for two for ever.'

'I'd be the size of an elephant if I did that and

be on a perpetual diet for the rest of my life.' The chocolate éclair was divine. Great choice. Thick and rich and moist. It slid very easily down her throat. 'But, listen, you never tell me properly about your trips. It's always *murky* or *dry* or *messy*. But it must be way more than that.'

Leaning back in his chair, he crossed his arms and watched her eat. His gaze wandered over her, causing a riot of goosebumps over her skin, and she stared right back. Splatters of cream paint stuck to his old grey T-shirt. Funny, she remembered buying that for him years ago at a gig she'd been to when he'd been covering the night shift. It had been a little baggy on him back then but now it barely contained his solid biceps and stretched across a chest of muscle. His hair was sticking up in odd places, and he was dusty.

His knuckles were scratched and his skin torn. He looked rugged and edgy and it was such a turn on to watch him move she could barely think straight. This was dangerous territory. Every second spent with him was pushing her closer to an edge she knew was going to be at once delicious and yet potentially soul-damagingly painful.

He took a sip of hot black coffee. He'd ordered

just that, no food. With wall-to-wall dessert on offer the man was clearly mad. 'So what exactly do you want to know?'

'What kinds of things do you get up to out in the field? The people you meet. I know you usually work at the tent cities, but what are the real cities like?'

His shoulders lifted in a sort of nonchalant shrug. 'The agency gang are pretty solid— people who want to do good, but all fed with a huge dose of reality. We know our limitations, there's never enough of anything—resources, people, help— but there's no point beating yourself up about what you can't achieve, you just get on and do what you can. While we're there the team always develops a huge bond, but such intensity can also drive you completely nuts. We do what we can in desolate and desperate parts of the world. There are, sadly, too many of them. But we do make a difference.'

'Well, there's no shortage of work, judging by the stories in the papers about floods, earthquakes and war zones. There's endless need for you everywhere.' He went to them all without any hesitation and she'd never once heard him utter one word of complaint about the harsh conditions he must have to endure, and the terrible things he must have seen. He kept everything tight inside him, but she didn't doubt he made a difference. He must have saved hundreds of lives and given thousands more help and much-needed hope. 'And the people you help? What are they like?'

'Desperate. Stoic. Honest. Victims. They have nothing apart from the clothes they stand up in. No homes, nowhere to call their own. There's always a threat—if it's not soldiers and fighting, or landmines and rogue devices, it's weather. Too much rain, or not enough. They need so much more than we can give them. But we fight to save their kids' lives. It's important to have a generation of hope that can break through the cycle of poverty and suffering.'

Pride rippled through her chest, her already tender heart bruising just a little more. Between him and her baby her emotions were being bumped around all over the place. 'But isn't it desperately heartbreaking? I know when I worked on the paeds oncology ward it damn near broke my heart.'

Again with the shrug. 'Of course, but it's uplifting too. You try to keep the emotion out of it, or you'd never survive. You can't carry all that and more around with you all the time, you just get on and do the job. I've learnt to detach.'

Hallelujah. 'Oh, yes. I've seen you detach, my friend. I have personal experience. You're pretty expert at it.'

'Yeah, well. I don't like getting in too deep.' He tried for a smile, which at once made him look boyish and yet very, very sexy. 'It brings me out in hives.'

'That much is obvious. You have form. Lots and lots of form. I'm thinking Sally the medical student, Jenny from Hamilton and Hannah the interior decorator. Poor Hannah, she was nice. You really broke her heart.'

'She was talking babies, mortgages, retirement homes…' He visibly shuddered. 'She had our whole future mapped out on the first date. And she even had a cutesie name for me. Seriously, one evening spent together and suddenly I was Macadoodle-doo. No one does that.'

Georgie couldn't help but smile. 'Oh, yes, they do. It's part of the relationship ritual. It's about creating a whole new world of two, developing a language you wouldn't speak to anyone else. I think it's endearing.'

'It isn't.'

She laughed. 'You know your trouble? You just need to let people in a little.'

'Really? My trouble?' His laugh was brief. 'My relationships have given you lots of entertainment over the years, missy, and vice versa. But I've never thought you had trouble that needed fixing. I just took you the way you are. I still do.'

'Even pregnant? Because that took a bit of getting used to, didn't it?'

His eyebrows rose and he let out a big breath. 'Yes, even pregnant. Look, things have been very weird since this whole pregnancy thing started, but I'm doing my best to deal with it.'

'I know you've been working really hard on the house. And it's been brilliant.' But he still had a damned long way to go—like talking about the baby unhindered, like being in the same room with her, like being able to look at the baby scans with joy instead of concern and fear, as if he expected pain.

Although the last day had proved he could spend some time with her. But with what consequences?

She'd almost dragged him to the bed the minute his breath had touched her neck. Holding back was the single most difficult thing she'd ever had to do.

Up until now she'd been the only woman he'd never detached from and it broke her heart to think she could well end up being just another one to add to his list. One kiss and they'd been on shaky ground ever since. Every movement he made, every space he filled, she was aware of him. Too much. Way too much. And that stunt in the bedroom had her flustered all over again. She was fighting the attraction but she didn't know how long she could hold out.

'I'm sorry. You're right. It's just…I can't help noticing that when you're struggling or getting close to someone you always cut loose right at the point when things start getting interesting. Like…' She wasn't sure of the wisdom of bringing this up, but if she didn't then he probably would anyway, if the conversation at the French market was anything to go by. 'Like earlier. Weird, but I really thought for a minute that you were going to kiss me.'

'Oh. That.' His mouth had been close to hers,

his raw masculinity emanating from every pore. She'd wanted him with a fierce and frightening urgency, had wanted him every day while he'd been up that ladder, flexing his arms to the ceiling, carrying timber around the house, hammering nails. Every. Damned. Nail. Each hit with the hammer had made her hot and bothered—and she was sure it wasn't good for her, or the baby, to have such a need that was being unfulfilled.

At what point, she wondered, did desire ever go away? Because for her it seemed to be getting worse by the minute, and just when she thought it was waning, he'd do something as simple as open a damned can of paint and just watching his hands move so confidently made her all hot and bothered again. Worse, the way he looked at her with such heat in his eyes made her believe he felt the same but that he was fighting it every step of the way.

But why?

Friendship. They had a decade of past and a long future hanging on the choices they made now.

There was a beat before he answered, as if he was debating what to say and how to say it, and she wished this situation hadn't made him so guarded. 'Georgie, make no mistake, I do want to kiss you, but I have just about enough self-control to hold myself back. It may not be a good idea to talk about this.'

'You did at the market.'

'That was before it had become a…habit.' He looked at his hands. They were still damned confident, even wrapped around a coffee cup, and she remembered what it had been like to feel so wanted as he'd hugged her.

'One kiss is hardly a habit.'

'Not the kiss. The wanting.'

'Ah.' Words were lost somehow between her throat and her mouth. The café sounds around her dimmed and her senses hyped up to acute overdrive. It was hard to breathe. Hard not to stare at those lips, those eyes, that face. Hard not to imagine what he could do to her and what she could do right back. Hell, he'd just admitted he wanted to do it again, so should she just kiss him anyway?

She felt like she was on a seesaw, her heart pulling one way, her head tugging the other. Up. Down. Up. Down. It was exhausting and exhilarating. With one look she could be flying, one word and she'd be hurtling back down to earth.

She struggled with her composure, but as always was falling deeper and deeper under his spell. And she could have struggled just a little bit harder, walked away, called a halt, but she didn't. Pure and simple. 'And why would you want to be so self-controlled?'

'Because it's too much to ask of us.' His eyes were burning with a sudden heat that felt as if it reached out and stroked her insides.

'We've already been through ten years. We already ask a lot of each other.'

'But now you're asking questions I don't know the answers to. You never did that before. You're trying to fix me and I don't need fixing. I don't want to be fixed. If we continue like this, things will change. Things have changed, and I'm not sure I like it, or want it, or know how to handle it, without letting you down.'

Part of her believed that to be right. He was being chivalrous and living up to his values, being honest about where things could or couldn't go for them. There was surely no future, especially with his emotional barriers. They were utterly and completely incompatible.

The other part of her wished he'd give up on his

good intentions and kiss her anyway. Because she could see neither outcome sat comfortably with him. Perhaps she should just make it easier for him. It wasn't as if she didn't know exactly what she was getting into. And if something didn't happen soon she would finally know what it was like to die from desire. *Fan the flames and let them burn out.*

'I've a feeling it's already a little late to worry about things changing between us. Don't you think? I'm not the only one here wondering what it would be like if we kissed again.' Pricking some vanilla cheesecake onto her fork, she offered it to him across the table. 'Don't you get just a little tired of being so saintly?'

'Yes. Every single moment I'm with you.' He leaned forward again and she was transfixed as he closed his mouth over the morsel of food. Heat shimmied through her as he very slowly chewed then swallowed, the movement of his Adam's apple dipping up and down strangely and compellingly sexy. Her eyes slid from his throat to his mouth, a guarded smile on a face filled with dips and curves she knew so well but had never really explored. How she wanted to trace her finger along those lips, to run her hand across his cheek and feel the rasp of his stubble against her skin. To scale the furrows of his cheekbones.

His voice was an octave dirtier when he spoke. 'My mind is working overtime, thinking of the things we could do together. But I'm sure it's just a passing phase. All interest in the new curves and stuff. I just want to touch you. It's a man thing— feral and protective and instinctive. We can't help it. Nature's a bitch sometimes. If we act on these instincts and then it doesn't work out, that's a lot of friendship down the drain. We need to co-parent on a platonic and sensible basis, not give in to rash lust and then have regret to deal with too.'

'Oh, so you mean the bigger boobs are distracting you? Interesting…' She very slightly arched her back as he lowered his gaze to her breasts. A powerful need zinged through her. She wanted him and was resorting to seduction of the clumsiest kind. But she couldn't get him out of her head. She needed to know what it would be like to be with him. If only one time. Just to hold each other as lovers, unlike the way they touched each other now, as friends. She wanted to stroke him, kiss every part of him. And if she didn't do it soon she'd go completely mad.

One day they'd look back on this and laugh. If they were still speaking to each other. 'So it's nature that's making you look at me like that?'

'Like what?'

'Sex.'

His pupils flared at the word. 'It'll wear off.'

'I sincerely hope not.' She finished the last bit of dessert in one big, almost but not quite satisfying mouthful. She had a feeling there was only one thing that could satisfy her right now, and it wasn't cheesecake. 'We should give in to our natural urges sometimes, it's bad for us to repress them all the time, apparently.'

'It's even worse to break something that's pretty solid.'

Their friendship. But that was true and lasting and proven. 'Why would it break? It doesn't have to break, not if we don't want it to. We can do whatever we want. It's our choice.' She couldn't resist stretching her fingers across the table towards his. For a few seconds just their fingertips touched. Then, without looking at her, he slid his fingers across hers, intertwined them, stroked his hand across hers. His skin was rough but his touch was soft. His heat spread through her, up her arms, to her back, down to her belly.

After a moment of such an excruciatingly sexy caress he turned her palm over and lifted it to his mouth. His kiss was hot. He licked a wet trail to her forefinger. She snatched her hand away before a moan erupted from her throat. Even so, her voice was filled with need. 'We should be getting home.'

'We? Is that an invitation?' His face cautious, and turned on at the same time, he scraped his chair back to go.

Finding him her sexiest smile, she whispered back, 'Honestly, Macadoodle-doo, since when have you ever needed an invitation to my house?'

'I think maybe this time I do.'

She hadn't answered him in words, but she'd taken his hand and led him out of the café like a woman on a mission. Thank God she lived only a short drive away because he couldn't have waited many moments longer. Liam didn't know when he'd ever been so burnt up about a woman.

They bypassed the living area and made it to

her bedroom without words, without kissing. He went in first, held open the door and she walked straight in and turned to face him, a question on her face. A dare. A promise. There was space between them. It would only need one step.

Just one.

He faltered. For a few moments neither moved as they stared at each other. This was happening. Really happening. The step from friends to…to whatever this was. *Lovers* might have been doubtful, but the trajectory from restaurant to street to bed was unstoppable. The air in the room seemed to still. One second. Two. With every lingering moment heat spread through his body like a raging fire, threatening to engulf him. If he touched her now there would be no going back.

This could have been a time to leave. He almost took a sideways step, his hand lingering on the doorhandle, but faltered again.

As she watched him a slow sexy smile appeared on Georgie's lips, and if he'd had any flicker of doubt that she didn't want this it fled right then. And that was when, he supposed, he should have drawn that line, the one they shouldn't have stepped over. Or where they should have agreed what this meant. But he was too consumed by her, by this need to utter a word.

In the end he didn't know who made the first move but suddenly she was in front of him, or he was in front of her and his mouth was hard against hers. This time there was no hesitation, no coy shaking. This was pure need and desire. She tasted of chocolate and vanilla and every flavour in between. Her mouth was wet and hungry and it fired a deeper, hotter want within him. Jaws clashed, tongues danced, teeth grazed. There was nothing sophisticated about the kiss, no gentle sucking or tender caress. It was messy. Dirty. Hungry.

His lips were on her throat as he dragged her T-shirt up around her neck, ripping it as it snagged on its journey to the floor. Finding what they wanted his hands cupped her beautiful breasts over her bra, then under her bra to the accompaniment of a deep guttural moan. She pressed against him, writhing against his thigh. 'Liam, oh, my God, I want you now.'

'I want you.' For a brief moment he acknowledged that this could be the singularly most stupid thing he'd ever done. Then that thought was gone, erased with more of her kisses and the press of her fingertips against the top of his jeans. He sucked in air as she played with his zip. And, no, he did not want to hesitate for a second—but his hand covered hers. 'You first.'

Her bra hit the floor and then her shorts, and he was walking her to her bed and laying her down on the flowery duvet he'd seen a hundred times before but never in this light, never at a moment like this. Everything was familiar and yet unfamiliar, like her. His mouth found her dark hard nipple and sucked it in. She was divine, so sexy, her nipples so responsive. *She* was so responsive as she writhed against him, nails digging into his back until he groaned.

As his mouth started its journey south, kissing carefully over the undulation of her belly, her hand stopped his and her voice was, for the first time, wary. 'Is this really stupid?'

'Without a doubt.'

'Yeah, I thought so. Dumb and then some.' Her mouth was swollen and red. He knew it had been a long time since Georgie had been kissed, and kissed like that—because he had been the last one to do it. God only knew when she'd last had sex but unless he was mistaken he could count the time in years, not months. So this was important. She'd chosen him.

He relieved her of her panties, hands skimming a belly that was plump and soft. He followed a trail of dark hair down her midline, watching her squirm as he parted her thighs and found her centre. He slipped a finger in, two, and felt her contract. She moaned, 'Oh, yes.'

'Crazy?'

'Madness.' She arched against him. 'But that feels so good.'

He kissed a slick trail to a nipple and smiled against it as she bucked in pleasure against his hand. Then he found her mouth again, her tongue tangling with his as she unzipped his jeans and took him in her hand. His gut contracted. He was so hard, so hot for her, and, damn, if he didn't have her soon he was going to explode.

She rubbed his erection against her sweet spot and he could feel the wet heat of her. Then she pushed him against the mattress and straddled him. 'I want you inside me, Liam. Now. Please don't do the whole slow build-up thing. That's been happening for days, months if we're honest.

I just need to feel you inside me. Otherwise I'm going to just about die.'

'Don't do that. No. We can't have that.' And without any further encouragement he slid deep into her. She was so ready for him, he could feel her orgasm building already, her walls contracting around him as she pulsed with him. She met his rhythm, found his mouth again and he was lost in sensation after sensation of her mouth, her centre, her weight on his thighs. Her scent around him, her heat around him. Deeper. Harder.

He wanted to slow down time, to hold onto this moment but the luscious heat of her, her sexy, knowing smile made him sink deep into her. 'Oh, my God, Georgie, you're going to make me lose it.'

He fisted her hair and dragged her face to him, kissing her long and hard until he was fighting for breath, until the pace increased, faster and faster. Her eyes closed as he felt her contract around him, her body shaking with the strength of her orgasm. *Liam. Liam.*

Never had his name sounded so sweet, so wanted, so precious. He was lost in her, in her voice, in her heat, grinding against her, hard and fast and deep, until he felt his own climax rising and then crashing on a wave of chaos and kisses.

For a few seconds she was quiet against him, Liam could feel her heart beating a frantic pulse against his chest. Her hair was over his face. She was covered in a fine sheen of sweat, fists still clinging to his shoulders, pinning him against the sheets. He was already hard again, thinking about a few moments' repose, then maybe a shower—preferably with her in it. It was startling, surprising and felt surreal to be here, with her, doing this.

So he wasn't prepared for her words as she bolted upright and her hand went to her belly. 'Oh, God, Liam. Oh, my God.'

The baby. For those fleeting moments he'd forgotten, blown away by the sultriness of her ripe body, of being inside her, of losing himself completely in the best sex of his life. He'd wanted Georgie the woman. Not Georgie the mother. Although she came as a package deal, he knew that.

No, he hadn't forgotten but blocked out that thought.

And then things got very murky in his head. 'What is it? Are you okay? What's wrong?'

'No, I'm not okay.' Twisting away from him, she climbed off his thighs, wrapped the top sheet across her front and curled onto the bed in a protective foetal position, her hands in front of her face. 'Oh, God, best-friend sex. Kill me now.'

'Why the hell would I want to do that?' The laugh erupting from his throat was part relief, part concern because she was right; in fact, they'd both been right. This was the most half-cocked stupid thing they'd ever done.

'I can't believe we've just done that when I look like this.' Her cheeks were red and hot. 'I've never cared how I looked to you before. You've seen me in all states of soberness and drunken debauchery, when I was sick, when I was glammed up to the nines. You've seen me lose my bikini completely in an ill-timed dive into the pool, even caught sight of me in my scaggy weekday bra and pants, and none of it mattered. Ever. But now? Now I'm so embarrassed.'

He stroked fingers down her spine, tenderness for her goofy display of embarrassment meshing with something else in his heart. This was not meant to happen. He was supposed to be creating a safe place for his child, proving he could be a good father. Making sound choices. It was okay to give in to a little sexual play with someone who had no strings attached—but they had a ten-year history and an uncertain and very shaky-looking future that involved another life. They shouldn't be playing at all. He was getting in too deep, getting himself into a situation he didn't know how to get out of. 'And maybe you're just a little bit crazy? Why do you think I care how you look?'

'Because it's suddenly important. Everything is. I didn't think it would be, but it matters.'

'I don't believe this.' Pulling her hands away from her face, he made sure she was looking right at him. Because, yes, this mattered. She mattered. Whatever else happened now—and already a thousand doubts were stampeding into his head—she had to hear what he was saying. Because she still needed to hear the truth, regardless of what he thought or felt about it. 'Is it enough for me to say that you're beautiful?'

'No. Not really. I'm six months pregnant, for goodness' sake. I'm fat. I'm getting stretch marks. My boobs are huge.'

'Really? I hadn't noticed.' He pretended to take a sneaky peek. And then wished that he hadn't.

He could make light of this, but the honest fact was she was beautiful. So beautiful it made his heart ache and he wanted to kiss her again, to make her scream with pleasure. To make her realise just how much she was wanted.

'Well, you've been staring at them for long enough.'

'That's because you are amazing. Beautiful. Fertile. Vibrant.' He took her hand, gently kissed her knuckles and brought her fist to his cheek. 'And I don't care how you look, Georgie. Because, honestly, the wrapping's not what I was making love to.'

Honestly? *Honestly?* His heart banged fiercely as if protesting. What the hell were they doing? She was his friend and by doing this he'd let her down. Period. He was supposed to be the strong one, dammit.

'You know, we should really have stopped before we started.' Dragging her hand from his grip, she sat up. 'If that makes sense.'

'Things stopped making sense a while ago.'

'Yes, you can say that again.' She let out a long sigh but snuggled against him, her hair tickling his nose, baby-soft skin touching his, then closed her eyes. 'That was good, though. Damned good, Macadoodle-doo.'

He glanced towards the bedside table and saw a baby name book, a pregnancy book. In the corner of the room there was a bottle steriliser still in its wrapper next to a bundle of baby clothes. On the floor to his left was a magazine open at a page about safety in online dating. She'd gone through the questionnaire and circled a few As, some Cs, a smattering of Bs. Was she thinking about dating again? Before all this she'd have filled in the questionnaire with him and they'd have been in fits of laughter at the results. But this one she'd done on her own. In private.

Despite the post-coital warm fuzzies he realised with a jolt that he might not be a real and integral part of her new life. She was thinking about a future without him in it. That was what he'd wanted, right? That was why he'd signed the contract in the first place. So she could have her dream life— a partner would be the icing on the cake for her. A husband, two kids and a dog. The family she'd missed out on, growing up in that children's home she'd hated. Traceable DNA.

A husband who didn't keep running away. She deserved that. She deserved the very best.

And even though he knew all the reasons he shouldn't be here, he still kept batting them away, trying to find good enough reasons to stay. But he didn't have many, apart from selfish ones that meant he got the best sex with an amazing woman and then broke both their hearts.

He edged his arm out from under her neck, lay for a few minutes and watched her. She looked so relaxed, so peaceful, so hot that he couldn't bear to think of her with another man. But did that mean he had to commit? What if it fell apart? That would be all kinds of messy. A family didn't need that. He didn't need that, and she certainly didn't. From his own bitter experience he knew damned well what damage a broken family could do to a child.

Better to stay friends for ever than fall apart as lovers.

Snaking away from her, he sat on the edge of the bed and looked around for his jeans. 'I guess I'd better get off home.'

'Oh, no. Don't you dare move, matey.' Her hands were on his shoulders, gripping them with more force than when he'd taken her over the edge, forcing him to sit back down. She picked up one of the books he'd seen and flicked through it, shoving it under his nose. 'So, I was thinking Desdemona for a girl. Albert for a boy? What do you think?'

'What? You're joking.' Not what he'd choose in a million years. What he would choose he didn't know. He hadn't allowed his mind to wander down that route as yet.

'And in the morning we need to go shopping for a breast pump. There's a new babyware shop opened up on High Street. And I know it's early but I want to get some Christmas decorations from that pop-up shop in Regents mall.'

'Christmas? Already? It's September.'

'My first Christmas in my first home. A baby on the way. I want it to be special.' Her voice was wistful. 'No harm in starting early, and they'll sell out of all the good stuff pretty quickly, you'll see.'

'What was Christmas like at the home?' He knew she tried to make a huge effort to celebrate it every year and asked everyone she'd ever met to eat around her large wooden table—waifs and strays, everyone's uncle's cat…she just didn't want to be on her own.

There was a pause as if she didn't want to go back there. He couldn't blame her. The bits she'd mentioned about growing up had been a far cry from his early experiences. Until his perfect world had imploded.

She put on her *I'm okay* voice. 'Oh, the social workers and carers tried to make it feel special, but we all knew they just wanted to get our celebrations out of the way so they could finish up and get home to their real families. It was depressing, in truth. This year I'm going to go big. I'm going to get the biggest tree and the most decorations anyone has ever had and cover the place— the tree, the walls, the outside. You know, like on Franklin Road, where every house has decorations and lights? It'll be like that, a Christmas to remember. And then next year I'm going to give Desdemona—or Albert—every damned thing they want. Because I couldn't have what I wanted. Ever.'

He imagined her, stuck in the home, wishing her little heart out and always being disappointed. Life sucked sometimes. For Georgie life had sucked a lot. 'What did you want, Geo? What did you wish for?'

'Ah, you know, the usual stuff.'

He propped himself up on his elbow and ran his fingers across her curves, down her shoulder, to the side of her breast, and stopped for a moment as she shivered under his touch. Then continued stroking her hip. 'No. Really, what did you want?'

She laughed, shyly. 'I wanted to start a collection of Beanie Babies—these little stuffed-toy things. Man, they were expensive and all the girls at school had them for birthdays or Christmas. I saved up my allowance every week and eventually bought a second-hand whale. He was my favourite.'

So he wasn't the only one here who was expert at dodging a question. 'No. Really. You're always telling me to stop hedging—but you're champion of it too. What did you deep down want?'

'Oh, God. However I say it, it's going to sound twee and crass but…well, I really wanted to be part of something. And now I am. So I got it in the end.' She laughed. 'It only took twenty-eight years.'

Did she mean him? Did she mean they were now part of something? Or did she mean the baby?

Family? His heart started to pound. What had he done? Given her hope that she belonged to him? Didn't she? No. No one did. No one could.

What the hell had he done? 'Oh. I see.'

'Anyway, before we go shopping I thought perhaps a big brunch in town first. That's what we'll need, right? A good sleep and then some decent food. Or maybe some food now? Are you hungry? Sex makes me hungry.'

'These days everything makes you hungry.' Okay. He got it that it would be rude and insensitive to split right now. He slumped against the pillow, trying to reconcile his head with his heart, but it seemed they were cursed to be at odds with each other for ever. 'Whatever you want.'

'Really?' Her foot dug him in the thigh. 'What I want is for you to stay. Talk to me.'

'God knows how you have the energy to talk after mind-blowing sex.' He ignored her assertion that he stay. For how long? Tonight? Tomorrow? A year? For ever? Reality was blurring dangerously with the ache in his heart.

One eye opened. 'It's not because we've just had sex, it's because *we* talk, Liam, that's what you and I do. We talk endlessly and have done for a decade. About everything. *Mostly.* We've never not known what to talk about before. How about we talk about stuff…about your work, my pregnancy, this child, your family, why you don't contact them ever? What the heck it is that spooks you so much about creating something that everyone else in the world craves. I want to know about you growing up, and I want to know about Lauren.'

The walls were closing in. It was time for evasive action, because he did not want to go there. At all. 'You know, suddenly I'm really fascinated about how breast pumps work. Talk me through—'

'No way, José. You don't get out of stuff that easily.'

'Oh, but I do. By fair means or foul…' The sheet covered most of her body, but her right foot was sticking out. He took it, leaned forward and slowly sucked her big toe into his mouth. He felt her soften against the mattress and her moan stoked more heat in him. That shower scenario was looking more and more attractive.

'Yeow. Definitely not fair.' Four vermilion-varnished toes wriggled against his chin. 'Use that mouth for talking, Macadoodle-doo.'

'Why, when it's so much better at doing other things?' His mouth hit her ankle, the back of her knee, her inner thigh, and he licked a wet trail northwards. As she squirmed he gave a wry smile. Any more wriggling was halted by his hands on her thighs. 'See?'

'But I want to— Oh, yes, that feels good. Just a little to the… Oh, yes.' Her hands fisted into his hair. 'Don't stop now, Liam…'

'I have no intention of stopping.'

'We…can…talk…later…'

Like never. 'Hush. Relax. Enjoy.'

And with that her mouth clamped shut and as he grasped her hand, she did exactly what he'd suggested.

CHAPTER NINE

WHEN GEORGIE WOKE the next morning the left side of the bed was cold. He was gone. As she'd thought he would be. It had all been too good to be true. He'd had second thoughts and hot-footed it to Afghanistan or somewhere equally unreachable. Typical Liam. Typical men. She lay back on the pillow and growled.

And then growled again, because since when had her mood been determined by a man?

Since Liam MacAllister had become...whatever he'd become. More than a friend...and with added and rather nice benefits. He certainly was very, very good at the bedroom side of things, even if he was quiet—*mute*—on the history side. But, hey, a forward-thinking man was always better than one looking back, right?

Although his past had shaped who he was, and that intrigued her. It had also created those barriers he was so keen at throwing up between himself and anyone who wanted to get close. The sex had been a really crazy idea. Lovely but crazy, and now she was even more confused than before. Ask him for clarification? Not likely. She imagined how that conversation might go and decided she didn't need to have him actually voice the rejection out loud.

After a few minutes of lying there, debating what to do, there was a gentle tapping at the door and in he walked, topless, with jeans slouching off his hips, a tray in hand, a pot of coffee and a plate of something that smelled nice but looked a little…suspect. He gave her a smile as he placed the tray on the bed. 'Morning. Here's a sad-looking croissant I found at the back of the freezer, along with a couple of rogue frozen peas and a lot of ice. There was literally nothing else to eat. Nothing. You really do need to go food shopping.'

'The trouble is I eat it as fast as I buy it. I can't keep up.' Without his shirt *he* looked good enough to eat—did she need anything else? And he hadn't run off, he was here, making sure she ate properly. Was this a dream?

She rubbed her eyes, which she really shouldn't have done because the corneal abrasion was still healing, but it was too late and… Yes, he was still here, not an apparition. With food. And coffee. The man was a god.

The god sat on the edge of the bed. 'Well, seeing as we're having a day off renovating today, I'll make sure we fill up the fridge before we're done.' He buttered a piece of croissant, offered it to her, then waited until she'd opened her mouth and popped it in. 'Come on, get your strength up, we're going to need that soon enough.'

'Thanks. Eugh. Not such a great croissant. I can't even remember when I bought— Wait… we're having a day off? Who says?'

'You said you wanted to go shopping. And I'm tired of sanding and painting and you look like you need a decent break. I want to forget about this dust and dirt and do something else. So I've made some calls. I have a plan: your breast pump will have to wait, along with the Christmas decorations. Eat up and then we'll get going.' He got up as if to leave.

'Not so fast.' She caught his hand and he took it, wrapped his fingers around hers and squeezed. In all the years of knowing him she'd never been aware of this tender side to him. She liked it.

Goddamn, she liked it, just when she was trying to think of more reasons not to like him. Not to lose her heart or herself to someone who wouldn't want it. 'To where?'

'It's a surprise. But there'll be proper fresh air. The sea. Decent food. No dust.'

'Is this just another tactic to avoid the issue? You know…talking?'

He gave her a guilty grin. 'I feel restless. I just need to get going. Out. Somewhere.'

This was the guy who spent most of his life travelling and the last few months cooped up in her house. He never stayed anywhere for long, so she could see why he'd need to cut loose sometimes. Plus, a break would be fun. 'Then what are we waiting for?'

'Well…' He pulled the sheet down a little and exposed her breasts. Then he kissed her neck, her throat, her nipples, and she was putting her arms around his neck and drawing him to her. He whispered against her skin, 'I really need a shower before I set foot outside. You?'

'What? Me and you? In that tiny bathroom? You think we'll fit?'

'If it's big enough for a highland jig, it's big

enough for a shared shower. We'll squeeze in somehow.' His fingers stroked down her back and she could see the bulge in his jeans. He was hot and hard for her.

Which made her hot in return. She couldn't resist reaching her hand to his chest. Felt his heart beating underneath her fingers. Solid. Steady. *Liam.* This was Liam. This was all kinds of surreal. She remembered his little dance in her tiny bathroom, the way he'd looked at her, the way she'd wanted to touch him then. How touching him now made her feel excited and jittery and turned on. Not solid or steady at all. 'But it wasn't big enough for a highland jig, remember?'

'We'll fit. Trust me?'

'I don't know.' That was half the problem. And, yes, he'd stuck to his words and been there for her throughout this pregnancy. Not once had he mentioned the contract again. He seemed committed to the baby, even though there were times when she caught his worried face and just knew the spooks were there, haunting him a little. But he'd surprised her with his resolve. And kept on surprising her, but could a man really change? She just didn't know. For a few minutes last night she'd thought he'd been having doubts, had felt his restless legs keen to leave, had known that if she'd let him he'd have gone. Would she always have to keep anchoring him here? Would she never be enough for his first instinct to be to want to stay?

For now, though, he was here and was asking for nothing more than to spend time with her. Time she didn't want to waste analysing things to death. 'Oh, okay. Where's there a will, there's always a way.'

'Always…' His laugh was deep and sexy and there was no way she was going to put up any kind of fight against those fingers, that mouth, those eyes. Had she been thinking about fighting? She couldn't remember. Her whole world narrowed to this single moment when she could forget everything else. 'So what are we waiting for?'

His hands closed around her fingers. 'Absolutely nothing.'

An hour and a half later, which truly could have been only thirty minutes had it not been for a lovely long shower and a very deliciously sexy start to her day, Georgie let out a yelp of excitement as Liam steered his expensive and very un-child-friendly two-seater coupé into a car ferry terminal. 'Waiheke Island? A day trip?'

'If that's okay?' He looked genuinely concerned that she was happy with his choice. 'I thought it'd be nice to do something different.'

'Yes, it's fabulous. It's a lovely idea. I haven't been there since a school trip years ago.'

He stared across at the ferry. 'My grandparents lived there, we used to go over and stay at their house every holiday when I was little. I can't remember the last time I visited.'

And there was something else she hadn't known about him. Maybe that concern on his face was really apprehension? 'Oh, I had no idea. Will it bring back bad memories for you?'

'I'm hoping to cement some new ones. It's a big enough island for me not to even go there.' A stream of vehicles appeared and queued up behind them as a crew member gestured for the cars to embark. Cranking the car into gear, Liam drove up the metal ramp and parked the car on the ferry platform. Once out, and breathing a lungful of fresh sea air, he slipped his hand into hers and whisked her towards the bar area. 'Come on, let's get a coffee and watch the world go by.'

The short journey across the Hauraki Gulf was smooth and pleasant, enhanced greatly by a pod of dolphins that came alongside to play. Diving and chasing and showing off, they added extra magic to this unexpected trip. Standing on deck, watching him walk towards her with two cups of coffee in his hands, grinning and gesticulating to the wildlife, Georgie's stomach gave a little hearty jump at the thought of a stolen day with Liam. Things were definitely changing, moving along in a direction she hadn't ever imagined. She didn't know if the changes were for the good, but she did know she would never be the same after all this.

Waiheke, famed for its vineyards and olive oil, was showing the tentative beginnings of the new spring season. After a long wet winter the hills were green, the acres of vines stretching on and on to the horizon were budding and leafy, while ewes watched over lambs in the fields adjacent to the roads. Once away from the main township they headed east along a winding road that eventually opened to vistas of clean empty beaches and blue water sparkling in the pale sunshine. Such a difference from her city house, which she adored—but stepping onto green fields would be nice for a change. Liam had been right, time out would do them both some good.

After half an hour or so he pulled left into a white gravel driveway that led towards the sea. On their right was a large whitewashed colonial house with a sign advertising wine sales and tastings. Georgie was surprised he'd pick a place like this. 'Oh? You booked us lunch at a vineyard? I assume you want to sample the wares?'

'I may have a small glass. But it's not so much the vineyard I was planning to see.' He threw the car into park and got out.

She stepped out of the door and sighed at the wisteria just starting to flower and framing the large wooden door. The soft pink against the white was startling and soothing, and like something from a film set. 'Oh? So what is it? What's the big secret?'

'It's not so big really, more a thought than a secret. Wait and see. And apparently they do a very nice lunch platter. It's huge. Which seems to be the only consideration you make these days when choosing meals.' There was a flurry of activity as their hosts found them a table out in the garden, bottled water and much-needed shade.

The garden was private and secluded, but felt somehow open rather than cloistered. Cushioned candy-striped hammocks hung between trees flanking a small neat square of grass. Palms and large ferns gave much-needed shade. There were fairy lights entwined around the vegetation that she imagined would give a pretty effect in the evenings, along with tealights in coloured glass jars on the ornate ironwork tables. It was tranquil, cool and very calming, and as they sat she felt some of the tensions of the last few months float away.

The menu was limited but sounded delicious. Suddenly she felt famished and so ordered a large mixed platter that promised fish, freshly cooked meats, a selection of local hard cheeses and lots and lots of bread. Most of which, she knew, she could eat and not worry about them having any effect on her baby. The rest she'd leave for Liam.

As they waited for the food he started to chat. 'Chris, the owner of this place, is an old school friend of mine. He inherited the vineyard from his dad and has turned it into a very successful business.'

As she listened to the sound of…nothing, except the fuzzy hum of bees and faint birdcalls, and took in the impossibly breathtaking surroundings, she felt the most peaceful she'd felt in weeks. Either that, or the sex-induced endorphins had made her limbs turn half to rubber. 'It's amazing.'

'Isn't it?'

'So what made you decide to come here of all places?'

'He sent me a link to his new website the other day. I took a look, saw the photos of the deck and the garden.'

They were momentarily interrupted as their drinks arrived, then were left alone again. Liam took a sip of pinot gris, then put his glass down on the table. 'Then, when I was standing on your deck this morning, looking out at the garden, I thought that we really need to sort it out. The wood's rotting in places and there are nails popping up all over. It's a wreck, Georgie, and could be dangerous if we don't do something about it. The inside of your house is almost complete now so I thought we should finish things off properly. The baby's coming in the summer, and with the usual Auckland humidity you're going to want to sit outside. I thought the hammock idea would be great. And the palms give great shade. A lawn in the middle would be a pretty cool place for a baby to learn to crawl—no risk of injury.'

'Well, wow. That's really thoughtful. And, yes, it's absolutely gorgeous. I can see it working perfectly in the space I have. That's very kind of you, and especially to bring us all the way out here to actually see it.' She felt a little as if the ground was shifting. Half hope, half…what?

He shrugged, looking a little embarrassed at her enthusiasm. 'It's just a day trip, Georgie.'

But it was one of the kindest things anyone had ever done for her. Why did he have to keep getting better and better? Why couldn't he slink off and make her feel unhappy and not pine for more? In cold, harsh reality she was scared that she'd get too attached to a man who would break her heart. Because even if he did want to be involved in her family, how could she be sure he'd be in it for the long term? With her? How could she be sure he'd love *her*?

'But it's—'

'Oh, here's lunch. And here's Chris. Clearly a busy man, he owns the place, makes the wine and so, it seems, serves the food.' He stood and shook the hand of a thickset man who looked older than Liam's thirty-two years. 'Good to see you, mate.'

'You too.' Liam's friend's eyes grazed over Georgie, down to her belly, and he beamed. 'And you must be Georgie. I'd know you anywhere, that social media's a beast, isn't it? You feel like you know people without ever meeting them.'

'Yes. Isn't it? Hello.' She may have been Liam's friend on any number of social network sites, but Georgie wondered how much Chris really knew and what Liam had said, if anything, about their unusual situation. After all, not many couples got pregnant first and then had sex. Everything was happening the wrong way round. Besides, the word 'couple' hadn't been breathed out of either of their lips.

They hadn't discussed yet what to say, if anything, to anyone who enquired about their situation. But as that seemed to be changing by the day, it was probably better that they hadn't come up with any definite description. Just Liam and Georgie, same as it ever had been.

Still, the winemaker seemed gentleman enough not to pry and diverted his gaze from her bump back to Liam. 'Look, I've got a bit of a rush on, can't stay and chat. Give my regards to your father, Mac. I hear he's retiring up north.'

Liam's eyebrows lifted. 'Oh? Really?'

It was his friend's turn to raise eyebrows. 'You didn't know?'

'I haven't caught up with him for a while.'

'No. He said as much last time he was over. He seemed a bit miffed. But, then, he always did. Are you going to pop over to The Pines?'

Liam shook his head. 'No. He sold it years ago. No point going backwards, is there?'

'I don't suppose so. Look, thanks for coming. Lunch is on the house. Good to see you.' Chris turned to leave then paused. 'Oh, make sure you try the syrah too. Delicious.'

Lunch was lovely, and as filling as Liam had promised, and Georgie ate as much as she could, managing almost the whole meal without mentioning the last conversation. But in the end it got the better of her. Her heart began to race as she brought up the difficult subject, so she tried to keep her voice level. 'So, when did you last talk to your dad?

Liam shrugged. 'I don't know. Two years ago?'

'*Two?*' It seemed nonsensical to have no communication with family members. If she—

'Look…' Pushing aside his empty plate, he let out a long breath. 'Please don't give me a lecture on how lucky I am to have a father and that I need to make the most of him. I know that's how you feel about families. But it isn't how I do.'

'But—'

'It's a lovely day. I really don't want to spoil things.'

'That may be a little late.' Although she knew she shouldn't have pushed it, he'd brought her out of a desire to help her, and to give her a rest. She was the one spoiling things.

For a moment she thought he was going to stamp or growl, but he fought with his emotions and put them back in that place that he never let anyone see. The man must have some ghosts, she thought, if he was so unwilling to talk. But he was tight-lipped about his work too—he kept everything tied in. Some people needed counselling, but he just wore it all in his skin, would never consider any kind of help, not even to get things straight in his head.

He saw that as a strength. 'Let's not do this

today, Geo. Let's enjoy ourselves, plan the garden, take a walk, anything but this. Talking about my family tends to put a huge downer on everything.'

'Okay.' But something niggled at her. Ate away at her gut. She was genuinely trying to help. 'Or we could say everything really quickly and get it out in the open.'

He shook his head with irritation, but he smiled. 'Or say nothing at all.'

'Or I could ask Chris.'

'He doesn't know everything.'

Now she knew she could leave it and walk away and pretend this conversation hadn't happened. Or she could take it a step further...hell, he knew everything about her. Everything. 'And I know nothing. When did you last see your mother? What is The Pines?'

'Okay, so we *are* doing this.'

She took a sharp breath and threw him her most winning smile. 'I see it as my duty as a friend to annoy you until you actually get to the nitty-gritty.'

'You don't have to take that role so much to heart, Georgie. Maybe the nitty-gritty isn't what you think it is.' He placed his napkin on the table and stood, offering her his hand, but he looked impatient rather than annoyed. 'The Pines was my grandad's house and I am resolutely not going there so don't even ask. Just don't. It's a no. There is no point going over stuff, it doesn't help. You can't change the past and some of it is best not remembered. And I last saw my mother on Mother's Day. I took her out for tea. And it was awkward as always.'

'No. You were in Pakistan, or South Sudan—somewhere. Either way, you weren't here. Make it the year before.' They walked out into the vineyard. Rows and rows of vines stretched before them on and on into the distance. They wandered aimlessly down a row, inhaling the smell of freshly mown grass. 'You know, Liam, your parents will be the only grandparents our child has. Seriously, they are the only other people in the whole world with a connection to him…or her. They are flesh and blood. I really wish you could try to make things work between you all. If not for anyone else's sake, for Nugget's.'

He shook his head. 'Sometimes I wish I didn't know you as well as I do, because then I wouldn't have to put up with this. Trouble is, I do know you and I know you won't give up. At all. Digging and digging.'

'It's what makes me such a good nurse, and why you love me.'

'Love?' He stopped short and stared at her. For too long. For so long she wondered what the heck was going on in his head. She closed her heart to his shocked question...*love?* She didn't want to know his answer. Or maybe it had always been there and she'd been afraid to look. But in the end he just shook his head. 'My parents divorced when I was ten, and neither of them have shown any interest in me since well before then. The feeling's mutual.'

'Why?'

'You really do want to do this, don't you?' He ran his fingers through his hair, opened his mouth, closed it. Opened it again. 'Because Lauren died. And rightly or wrongly we all blame me.'

'Why? What on earth happened? What could you have done that was so bad?' Over the years Georgie had pondered this. She knew his sister had died, knew his parents were separated. But piecing the bits together had been like trying to do a jigsaw with no picture as reference.

They walked in silence to the very end of the row and onwards towards the ocean, found a crop of rocks in the little bay and sat on them. A breeze had whipped up, but the sun still cast a warm glow over them. Even so, Georgie shivered at the look haunting Liam's face. The dark shadows were back. His shoulders hunched a little. He'd already let go of her hand and even though they were sitting side by side it seemed almost as if he'd retreated within himself.

His voice was low when he finally spoke. 'She was a premmie, born at thirty weeks, and had a struggle, but she finally got discharged home. She was doing well. She was amazing. Really amazing. The light of our lives.'

Georgie sensed something terrible was coming. She laid a hand on his shoulder and waited, holding her breath. The sound of waves crashing onto the shore was the only thing that broke another prolonged silence. That, and her heartbeat pounding in her ears.

'I caught a winter bug. Nothing serious, just a stupid cough, fever and a snotty nose that laid me low for a few days, one of those that most kids get. Mum banned me from being near her.

Very sensible, in hindsight. I just thought she was being mean.'

He looked like he wanted to continue but couldn't find words. When he composed himself enough to speak his voice was cracked and barely more than a whisper, 'But Lauren was so fascinating, such a little puzzle of noises and sounds with an achingly beautiful smile, that, as an eight-year-old big brother with a strong sense of responsibility and a lot of curiosity, I didn't want to keep away. So one morning when she was crying I sneaked into her room and picked her up, soothed her back to sleep. I held her for ages, I don't know how long, but long enough for her to go to sleep and for me to care enough not to wake her, so I held her some more.

'A few days later she came down with the same bad bug, but she couldn't fight it off. She tried, though. Tried damned hard. But she just wasn't strong enough.'

He hauled in air and stood, hands in pockets, looking out to sea. So alone and lost that it almost broke Georgie in two. She imagined what it must have been like for a young boy to go through something like that, and her heart twisted in pain.

He'd been doing what he'd thought was the right thing. Not knowing how wrong it could be. But the baby could have caught a bug anywhere—in a shop, at the doctor's surgery, in a playgroup. It had been bad luck she'd caught it from her brother. Bad luck that had kept him in some kind of emotional prison for the rest of his life.

At least, Georgie thought, she hadn't had something and then lost it. She just hadn't had anything at all, and in some ways that seemed almost preferable to suffering the way Liam had. Again she couldn't think of anything helpful to say, and couldn't have managed many words even if she'd known some formulaic platitudes that might have helped. Her throat was raw and filled with an almost tangible sorrow for him. 'I'm so sorry, Liam.'

'To cut to the chase, my parents were never the same after that. Eventually the grief was too much for their marriage. I got lost in the slipstream of guilt and blame. We've all rarely spoken since, doing only the perfunctory family necessities, if that. I suppose you could say it's pretty damned loveless.'

No. *He* was loveless. Losing his sister and then

being neglected by grieving parents must have been almost unbearable, especially countered by a flimsy excuse that it had all somehow been his fault. He'd been a child too, for goodness' sake. How could you lay blame on someone who only wanted to give a baby more love?

Georgie knew Liam well enough to know there was little point in trying to convince him that he was anything other than culpable. If he didn't believe it himself, and if his parents, the people who mattered, had never tried to reassure him, then what would her words mean to him?

But she stepped forward and wrapped her arms around his waist, hoping that somehow the physical sensation of her touch might convey her empathy for him in a way that words never could. 'And that's why you fight so hard year after year to save all those babies in those disaster-stricken countries.'

'They just need a chance. I can't right any wrongs and I can't wave a magic wand but I can give them real help.'

'And that's also why you don't want a family of your own.'

'Yeah, I didn't do so well with mine. Lauren

dying was hard going, but you get through it. Somehow. Eventually. But what I needed most was help, support, love. And I got nothing. Families can hurt you so badly. I wouldn't want to do that to any child of mine. Worse, judging by my experiences, I'd probably do more harm than good.' He shook his head, shook himself free of her grip, and walked back towards the vines.

'No. You're going to be a great dad.'

He pulled up to a halt. 'Really? You think? After what I just told you? I don't want to go through anything like that again. I don't think I'd survive it. I don't want to…' He started to walk again. Head down. Shoulders hunched.

She kept a few feet behind him, giving him the space he clearly craved. 'To what?'

'To lose something like that again.'

'You wouldn't.'

He railed round at her. 'How can you be sure? How can you stand there and make promises no one can keep?'

It was all so clear now. His idea of family was broken. His image of love was filled with so many negative connotations he couldn't dare risk himself again with that emotion. That was why she'd found him so distraught that first day she'd met him—caring for a sick baby had diminished him, reminded him of what he'd lost. But he'd taken that loss and turned it into his vocation. Not many could do that. Not many would face their fears every day.

Although he never let it get personal. He never let anything get to him. Ever. That was what the death of his sister had taught him, to keep everything and everyone at a safe distance. So he wouldn't feel responsible, so he wouldn't have to face the prospect of more pain if things got sticky. Hell, she'd been watching him do it for years, and had never felt how much it mattered. But now, *God*, now it mattered.

And still she was left only with questions. If that was how he felt, why had he torn up the contract? Was this all just some duty kick he was getting?

What would become of them all?

Sometimes she wished she had a crystal ball and could look into her future and see how it all worked out. But this time she was afraid. Afraid that what she'd see wasn't what she wanted.

She left him to meander through the vineyard, stopping to look at the tight fists of bright red buds at the end of each row, gathering strength to grow into flourishing roses, and to watch tiny white butterflies skitter past. And as they walked she noticed his shoulders begin to relax again. The sunshine and quietness chased the shadows away and eventually he came back to her, took her hand in his and walked towards a cluster of old stone buildings.

But before they left the vines Georgie paused and looked at the tiny fruit gripping tightly onto ancient gnarled wood. 'Do you think Chris would mind if we tried one of the grapes?'

He laughed. 'I think he probably would, but they're not remotely ripe anyway. They'll make our stomachs hurt.'

'But they're award winning, it said so on a big certificate on the wall back at the restaurant. Should we try? I've never had anything award winning straight off the vine before. How about you? You should try one.'

'No.' He pulled her hand away from the plant and hauled her against him. His eyes were hungry, his breathing quickened as he looked into her face, at her eyes, at her mouth. He was a complex man filled with conflicting emotions—but that didn't make her want him less. He was real and, yes, he was complicated. He was layered and that was what made him all the more intriguing.

He cupped her face and stared into it, his expression a mix of heat and fun and affection. Then he pressed his mouth to hers and kissed her hard. It was a kiss filled with need, with deep and genuine desire. This was new, this…trust, this depth, sharing his worse times and dark past. It was intense and it was raw but Georgie felt a shift of understanding to a new level. A new need. His grip on her back was strong as he held her and for a few moments she thought he would never let her go. And, holding him tight against her, she wished that very same thing with every ounce of her soul.

'Can I drive the car? Please?' Georgie grabbed the keys from Liam's hand and he let her take them. Let her run to his pride and joy and take the driver's seat, which he would never ever normally do. But, well hell, just telling her about his old life had set something free from his chest. He felt strangely lighter, freed up a little.

But then, as he climbed in beside her, his gaze flicked to her belly and there was that hitch again, the one that reminded him that happiness was always fleeting. That love could hurt just as much as it could give joy. He'd thought he'd be able to distance himself emotionally from her, and from the baby, but in reality the feelings just kept hurtling at his rib cage, ripping his breaths away, one after the other. Hard and fast until he didn't think he'd ever be able to breathe properly again. He didn't know whether to run away from her or keep a tight grip. But staying close opened them all up to him wreaking havoc again.

'Where are you going to drive to? Palm Beach is nice. There are some good shops in Oneroa. Or we could go for a walk along Rocky Bay.'

She ran her fingers over the leather steering wheel. 'No. I remember from my school history classes that there are tunnels somewhere left over from the Second World War. Do you know anything about them?'

'Stony Batter tunnels? Sure. My grandfather helped build them actually. He was born here, camped in the fields just up past Man O' War Bay through the last years of the war.' Sheesh, he'd opened his mouth and now he couldn't stop his past pouring out. 'He used to take me up there when I was a kid.'

She flicked the ignition and drove back towards the main road. 'Do you want to take a look?'

Did he? That would mean a drive past The Pines and a whole lot more memories. The weeks they'd spent here as a real family. Complete. God, why had he decided to come here to relive everything again? Why? Because, for some reason, Georgie made him feel as if anything was possible. Even overcoming a dark and murky past. Who knew, maybe he could squeeze his eyes shut as they drove past The Pines and he wouldn't feel the dread already stealing up his spine. 'Okay. If you insist.'

'I do.'

But that was a mistake. Memories joined the swirl of pain in his chest as they closed the kilometres between the vineyard and his old holiday home. Part of him wanted to grab the steering wheel and head straight back to the ferry terminal. But it was too late.

The Pines stood tall and dark and ominous as they drove past, the short driveway leading to the front door, still painted dark blue, ancient pohutakawa trees flanking the lawn, laundry flapping on the line, all gave his gut a strange kick. Memories of happier times filtered into his head—his father swinging him round and round, his mother laughing at their antics and calling them for dinner. The long leisurely Christmas lunches filled with fun and excitement—midnight mass, waiting for Santa, opening presents on Christmas Day morning.

They had been happy, once upon a time. But once that dream had been shattered, it had never been possible to reach that state again.

He let his gaze wander, turning his head slightly as the large rambling house went out of view. Glancing at him, Georgie jerked the car to a halt. 'That was it, wasn't it? The house?'

There was no point lying. 'Yes. It looks as if someone is renovating it.'

'Do you want to go and take a look?' Her eyes were kind as they settled on him and he knew she was trying to do the right thing by making him confront his demons. But he didn't need to do that here, he confronted them most days as it was. 'I'll come with you, you won't be on your own.'

'Let's keep driving.'

'Actually, no.' She drew up at the side of the road and before he could stop her she'd done a U-turn and they were back at the house.

'Georgie, I know what you're trying to do. It's okay. I'm fine. Things are fine.'

'Sure. If you say that enough times you might just believe it. I, however, take a little more convincing. Come on.' She stepped out, leaned against the car and wrapped her arms around her chest as she stared at the house. 'I can imagine you playing there in the garden. Causing mayhem. It's a real family home. Three generations all together. Nice.'

'It was once.' He wrenched himself out of the car and looked over at the house, fighting the tightness in his throat. 'The last time I was here was for my grandad's funeral.'

She turned to him, hair blowing wildly in the sudden breeze. 'I'm so sorry.'

'He lived here all his life, he loved the place, said he didn't need to go anywhere else.'

'It's nice that you have family history. It must be reassuring to hear about the past, thinking that your grandad walked along these same paths as you. It gives a connection, doesn't it?' Slipping her hand into his, she left it at that. But her words kept coming back to him as they walked across the road past the house and looked out over the bay towards the tiny islands dotted around the horizon.

Liam remembered his grandad telling him about the antics he and his mates had got up to here on the island—fishing, drinking, farming. How he'd courted Liam's grandmother for two years but had always known he'd marry her. How they'd devoted years of their lives to the community here. Liam had always known his ties to this place but it had been too easy to take them for granted. Then he'd tried to put as much space between him and them as he could.

He looked at Georgie now in profile, those gorgeous lush curls whipping in the wind; she would never know if they came from her mother's side or her father's. Those soft brown eyes—a hint of Maori blood? Italian? Again, she'd never know. That staunch tilt of the jaw—well, that was pure Georgie, from years of forging her independence and stamping her place in this world. How she'd turned her life into such a success from her rocky beginnings, he would always wonder at. She had no memories of any kind of family time, good or bad, no special Christmases, no history to talk of, no stories to tell her baby.

Nugget.

Fear washed through him. Fear and hope mingling into a mish-mash of chaos in his gut. He was going to be a father.

He was going to have to create memories for his child too. A history. And a future.

See, this was why he'd been against families for so long. Because the unbearable weight of responsibility meant you had to stop hiding yourself and be someone good. Deep down good. Unselfishly open and honest. You had to let go of the past and be that person, the one everyone relied on. The one everyone looked up to. The one who knew there was danger and risk in opening his heart, but did it anyway.

Trouble was, he just didn't know if he could be that man.

CHAPTER TEN

One month ago...

TIME WAS MOVING FAST. Too fast.

The next few weeks were a blur of sensual love-making and laughter. It seemed, to Georgie at least, that sex could be a good mix with friendship after all. Liam was still funny and helpful, he still hammered nails and painted walls. He made her laugh and sigh with delight. They chatted and joked about pretty much everything, as ever—and it seemed almost as if something inside him had been set free.

Except…there was that nagging worry that things were rattling towards an abrupt end. And there was still a part of himself that he held back, that she couldn't break through.

Georgie's head was in a state of flux. She didn't know what he wanted, and she wasn't sure what she wanted out of this either. There'd been no discussion of expectations and she was too scared to ask him about…*what next*. All she knew was that having him in her bed and by her side made her feel the very best she'd ever felt. Although she'd never again mentioned his past, she also didn't want to discuss a future.

Because for the immediate future—which in her terms amounted to the next eighteen years—she wanted what she had never had: a stable, loving environment for her child. She wanted her baby to feel loved and nurtured, as if it were the centre of the universe and not, like her, alone and un-wanted. She wanted her child to not have to fight every day to be noticed. She wanted her child to feel completely and utterly confident and…loved. Just loved.

So, in reality, she needed to forget about any kind of intimacy with Liam, shouldn't waste pre-cious time wondering how it was going to work out—because she should be concentrating on get-ting through the pregnancy and planning to bring up a child as a co-parent with a friend.

Which didn't work so well for her when she was lying next to him in bed, or trying to do the nine-to-five at her day job when her head was full of naked images of him earlier that morning.

'Georgie, did you manage to get the blood-test results for Kate Holland? She's coming in this afternoon and I want to make sure she's all set.' Malcolm had returned from settling his mum into a nursing home in Dorset and had hit the clinic with renewed vigour.

Georgie watched as he bustled around the office, ordered and officious. He was a nice guy, but had some traits that she found just a little irritating. In retrospect it was good that she hadn't asked him to be the donor for her child. What on earth had she been thinking? But, then, on the other hand, Malcolm was nice. Just nice. Not anything else. Not complicated, not sexy as all hell, not a brilliant kisser—okay, so she didn't know that, but he didn't have sexy lips.

'Georgie?'

Malcolm. He was sitting at the desk opposite her now, face masked by a computer screen. 'Oh, sorry. Yes?'

'Blood results for Kate Holland?'

'Yes, I phoned the lab to chase them again an hour ago and they said they'd email them through.

They should be here...' She tapped on her keyboard and brought the work up on screen. 'There you go. I've directed them to her file. All looking good. She'll be pleased.'

'Thanks.' Her boss's head popped up over the monitor. 'Georgie, are you okay?'

'Absolutely fine, thanks.' And so far she hadn't let her thoughts interfere with her job, but they were definitely trying to filter in. Which was annoying in the extreme, because she loved this job, needed the pay, loved helping people reach their dreams, so *focus* was the watchword of the day.

'If you need to talk anything through I'd be more than happy...' Malcolm's face disappeared back behind the computer screen, but after a few moments it reappeared again. 'No pressure, though.'

'Seriously, I'm fine. Tired, but that's to be expected.' And in truth the lack of sleep wasn't all pregnancy related.

Malcolm looked hugely relieved at the prospect of not having a stressing-out employee on his hands. She hadn't mentioned to anyone at work who the father was and wanted to keep things quiet. It was far too complicated to try talking about this kind of thing here. Everyone thought they knew everything, everyone thought they understood and they were all so lovely and well meaning, but how could they understand when she didn't even understand half of it herself?

Malcolm went back to tapping on the keyboard. 'Ah, I see we have Jo Kinney arriving in ten minutes for follicular monitoring.'

'I know, I made the booking, but don't worry— I'll make myself scarce. I understand how frustrating it is to see pregnant tummies in a fertility clinic when you're struggling to get even a fraction of the way.'

Her boss's voice was concerned. 'I'm hoping the counselling sessions are helping her.'

'I think so. The last time she was in she confessed to feelings of uncontrollable jealousy if any of her friends told her they were pregnant. And she's not talking to her sister at the moment because she's carrying twins. It's all so very difficult for her.' Since she'd become pregnant Georgie had been at pains to make sure she'd been extra-compassionate with her patients. She had what many of them only dreamt about and that was something she would never take for granted. 'I do have a feeling that she'll get there in the end, though.'

'We can only hope so. Don't look so worried, I'll give her the best shot we have.' Malcolm stood to leave. 'So do me a favour and take a lunch break for a change. The sun's shining and the yachts are racing out on the gulf. Get some fresh air. And while you're out, buy some tinsel, we need to Christmas this place up a bit, and last year's decorations are looking a bit sad.'

'Now you've definitely asked the right person for that job. I don't need to be asked twice to go Christmas shopping.' Smiling, Georgie stood and took off her name badge. She had plans to meet Liam for lunch, but had kept that information under wraps. Meeting him in secret for snatched lunches added to the excitement. 'Actually, I'm also going to go and take a sneak peek at that new baby shop. They import things from Europe apparently, it sounds wonderful.'

'Don't go buying the whole place up.'

'I won't. I'm just going for ideas. After the renovations I don't have much left over for the frills.' She grabbed her bag and made a quick mental list of things she needed. A pram, a cot, cloth nappies, a stroller. Basically, the essentials. It was only window shopping, but it was lovely to dream.

The light warm breeze was welcome after the cloistered atmosphere in the clinic. Summer was edging in and starting to make its presence felt; the shoppers and office workers on High Street had shed their thick woollen coats and knee-length boots. The shop displays had Christmassy reds, greens and silvers instead of wintry blacks and browns, Georgie noted, and that made her feel bright. Despite not knowing which way was up with Liam, there was so much she should be thankful for. She had a great house, a great job with understanding and supportive colleagues. She had a future right here in her belly. There were many not so fortunate.

She almost broke into song, with the buskers churning out the old Christmas favourites…and, strangely, hearing 'Away In A Manger' brought a lump to her throat. A happy lump.

Choosing a colour theme for her tree this year was hard, but in the end she went with traditional red and gold. A few new baubles. And a named one for her and one for Liam. And for Nugget too… Desdemona didn't fit.

The baby shop was exclusive and expensive, she could see that just from the window displays with beautiful hand-carved cots and no price tags. When she entered the well-dressed shop assistants greeted her with expectant smiles.

'Just looking, thanks,' she answered their questioning faces, and wondered whether she'd have been better walking past and on to the more affordable chain stores further down the road. But, oh, it was such an adorable place, decorated with luxury Christmas items—'Baby's First Christmas' bibs, blankets, towels. Miniature stockings hung from a makeshift mantelpiece. She eyed a kit for a hand-sewn advent calendar and made a mental note to add it to her ever-growing list. That would all have to wait until next year. Nugget's real first Christmas, and she'd make sure everything would be just perfect.

No, this Christmas would be special too. She had the feeling that waddling around trying to feed an army would be too much for her this year, so it would be just her and Liam, if she could lure him away from that ER…for the first time in her adult life she'd have a quiet one. At the thought of just the two of them spending such a special day together she grew a little hot. She imagined waking up to a special Liam Christmas surprise…and her cheeks flushed.

But where was he?

Clearly, he'd been held up by some emergency or other, but soon she'd need to get back to work, so she headed for the exit.

'Georgie? Hey, is that you, Georgie? Wow! Look at you. I had no idea…' It was Kate and Mark Holland, hand in hand staring into the same shop window.

'Kate?' The woman looked a darned sight healthier than she'd looked before, when she'd been bloated and on bed rest and pretty damned miserable. 'Lovely to see you. How are you doing?'

Kate's eyes twinkled. 'Not as well as you, clearly. My goodness, this is a surprise. When are you due?'

Georgie resisted running her hand over her now huge bump. 'Eight more weeks, end of January. A summer baby. Believe me, I am not looking forward to waddling around in that humidity.'

'Do you know the gender? What about names?'

More things on her list. She'd been putting off talking to Liam about names again, and when she'd jokingly mentioned it he'd ended up…well… it had been very nice indeed. 'No, I don't know the sex, I want it to be a surprise. And names are so hard to choose, don't you think? Picking one's hard enough, but a middle name too? That's all kinds of heavy-duty responsibility. Imagine picking a name and them hating it for the rest of their lives.'

'So you have some planning to do. I like the traditional ones myself. Make a list.' Kate seemed genuinely pleased for her and wrapped her in a gentle hug. 'Lucky you. I really am pleased.'

Georgie told herself to get a grip as her throat filled with emotion for Kate. Her hormones were all over the place today. 'I saw you'd booked into the clinic this afternoon—what's the plan?'

Her patient gripped her husband's hand as they both smiled. 'My mum's given us some money for one more round, an early and very unexpected Christmas present. I can't tell you how amazing that is. I just can't give up. I just can't.'

'That's great news. Really brilliant. I'll keep everything crossed for you and we'll do everything we can at the clinic.' Georgie knew exactly how Kate felt and wondered just how hard she'd have fought to feel the way she felt right now. Hell, she'd have kept on fighting until she'd had no fight left. And then she'd have fought harder still. Nothing was as precious as this child, getting this child. Having this child. It was the first time that Georgie had ever sensed what it would be like to be part of a family. To belong. To love and be loved, unconditionally. And Liam fitted into that picture too. No matter how much she tried not to, she couldn't help but do some serious Christmas wishing on that account.

'Thanks.' Kate bit her lip and her eyes briefly fluttered closed. 'I'm a bit worried, to be honest. I don't want to have another major disaster like last time.'

'Okay, so the first thing you have to do is stop worrying. That's not going to help at all. We'll start you on a lower dose of stimulation drugs this time and monitor you very closely. There's nothing to say that you'll have the same experience again. Really, try to relax, that's the best thing you can do. I'll see you later and we can talk more then.'

'Okay. See you soon.'

Georgie was about to leave when she felt a

prickling along her neckline. Turning, she saw Liam approaching and felt the immediate rush of bright light whenever she saw him. 'Hey. Did you forget the time?'

'I'm so sorry. Just one thing after another today.' He shook his head and pecked a kiss on her cheek. 'Did I miss the shopping? Come on, let's go. I'm starving.'

'Me too.'

He grinned. 'No surprises there. What's in the bags?'

She hid the bag of named baubles behind her back and grinned right back—he'd probably think she was just a sentimental old sook. 'Not telling.'

'Aw…come on.' As he spoke his mobile phone went off. He shook his head in irritation, dragged his phone out of his pocket and looked at the display. 'Look, I've got to get this.'

'Who is it?'

'Just MAI.'

'The agency? Why? What do they want?' She felt the colour drain from her face. He'd been home so long this time. Long nights she'd kept him to herself like a delicious secret, always knowing that this day might come but pretending that it wouldn't. Convincing herself that it wouldn't matter anyway, that she was on top of her feelings about him. She'd managed to leave herself enough space and hadn't fallen for him so completely that his leaving would damage her.

Besides, he didn't have to go. The baby was due soon. He would turn them down. He would stay. 'What do they want?'

'No idea.' He shrugged. 'Sorry again. I won't be long.'

He turned a little away from her and she stared into the shop window, half looking at the too-expensive wares, half-listening to his side of the conversation. It would be fine. She would be fine. He wouldn't run, she trusted that he wouldn't go now, not when she needed him.

'Hey. No worries. Where…? How long…? Why…? What do you need?' Suddenly his voice went quiet and the bright light inside her went out.

He stayed quiet for a few moments as he listened to the caller. Then he looked over and caught her eye. There was something about his tense expression that made her heart stumble. Guilt? Panic? He tried for a smile, but it was more regretful than reassuring. Then he closed his eyes, turned his back to her, shoulders hitched.

Something was wrong.

She strained to listen, but whether he was hiding the information from her or protecting her she didn't know.

She heard her name.

She heard 'pregnant'.

She heard, 'Yes, I'll do it.'

Then he stood stock-still.

Something was wrong. Numbness crept through her. The only things she could feel were the fast, unsteady beat of her heart and the clench of her fists around the shopping bag handles.

Something was wrong but, unlike her house, or the garden or the zillion things that had broken over the last few years, Liam wasn't going to fix this.

Liam snapped the phone into his pocket and turned to face her, already understanding that she'd heard a little and assumed a lot. Things were careering out of control in every direction he turned. 'I'm sorry. Again.' It was inadequate, he knew, but it was heartfelt.

'So you keep saying. What for? Being late for lunch or agreeing to whatever it was you just agreed to?' Her eyes were dark, her cheeks hollowed. She knew him too well, Liam realised. He couldn't hide things from her. 'What did they want? No…more to the point, when are you leaving? Where are you going?'

'Sudan. Tonight.'

'They need you, right? There's no one else? Absolutely no one else? Tell me they were desperate. You had no choice?'

The pause he gave was too long. Long enough for her to read between the lines. They'd sort of asked and he'd sort of offered. And, yes, there were others who could have gone. He'd just fast-tracked himself to the top of the list.

Things between them had got so complicated so quickly, he was thrashing around trying to make sense of it. But he couldn't.

Yes, he loved waking up with her. Yes, he loved spending time with her. Too much. It was all too much and he was starting to want things, to feel things he shouldn't about the baby and about her. He was supposed to have kept his emotions out of all this and yet here they were washing through him. Guilt. Panic. Adoration. Need. *Fear.*

And taking that risk was a step too far. He needed to get his head straight. To have time to think. Sudan was the perfect place. It wouldn't be for ever, but it might just be enough to get things in order again, so he could be rational and stop these gut-wrenching emotions messing with his head. 'Well…'

He could hardly look at her, but he had to face her anger.

Which was swift and fierce and almost tangible. He could see her starting to close down.

She shook her head and strode past him. 'Okay. So you've made your decision. I have to go to work. I'm going to be late.'

Liam followed her down Queen Street towards her clinic, trying to keep up. The way she'd looked at him he could have sworn she'd wanted him to say something more. Something profound. But he wouldn't lie to her, let her think one thing, believe something—*want* something—that he wasn't sure he could give. Hell, she was hearts and flowers all the way and he was, in comparison, a lost cause. He shouldn't have let things get to this point. 'For a woman who's seven months pregnant you can sure keep a good pace.'

'That's because I'm in a hurry. My clinic's due to start and you're making me late for *my* job. You're not the only one with a strong work ethic.' She was in front of him now, grumping over her shoulder. And watching her stalk ahead, all proud and indignant, made him want her more. Which gave him every reason why he should get that damn flight.

'Georgie, we need to talk about this.'

'Really? You think?' She stopped outside the clinic. 'When you've already made your decision? You jumped at the chance. No hesitation. I didn't see much talking going on between us.'

He followed her up the stairs and into a meeting room. He closed the door and went to sit opposite her across a table. The table was too big, the room too sterile.

Her words echoed off the walls. 'And you don't know for how long. You never do. It could be months.'

'Look, it'll be okay. Everything will be fine. The deck's almost finished, the garden just needs some final touches. Don't do anything until I get back.'

Those lifeless eyes regained a spark that flamed. 'So this is your idea of being in it for ever? A lifetime commitment, and this is what you're promising? You won't be here geographically—and I can probably handle that. A lot of mothers have to deal with that. But...oh, this is unfair. I'm being unfair.' She stood up. 'I knew this all along, but—'

'What? Say it... Say what you're thinking.' He reached across for her hand, but she pulled it away. She was closing down. 'Talk to me, Georgie.'

'What's the point?'

'It's what we do. Talking.'

'Not, it appears, about the important things. Not when it matters. You should have discussed it with me first. *We* should have decided.' She took a deep breath and huffed it out. 'You say you're committed, that you want to work as a team, as a co-parent, but the moment they call, you jump. *You* choose. You can say no. You can stay here. There is a get-out clause. I do know.'

It was important that he remain calm and let her anger bounce off him. 'It's my job, Georgie. I've been home for a long time.' *Home.* That thought made Liam's stomach clench— it was the first time he'd thought of anywhere as home. Georgie's home. His heart swelled in pride at what they'd achieved at her house, but simultaneously he felt as if it was being slashed into pieces. 'This will be the last time. I'll make sure I resign completely after this.'

'I'm sure that's what they all say, and I'm sure they mean it too. Besides, I know why you do it, month after month, serving your penance to Lauren. I get that. I wouldn't ask you to give it up. But now? Right now? When you have a choice and you chose them. You chose them. Unbelievable.' She began to pace the room, glancing every few seconds at the clock. Which ticked away the minutes sonorously, ominously, like a sentinel counting down.

She stopped walking. Her hands gripped the back of a chair. There was a small hole in the dark grey fabric, the edges frayed. She seemed to stare at it as she spoke. 'So you told them? About the baby?'

'Yes.'

'And you might not be here for the birth?'

'They said they'd try to make it happen.' The

ache that had started in his throat seeped into his chest, getting more raw and more real.

Distance. That's what they needed, then they'd be able to think and talk and act rationally, without the sideshow of pumping hearts and that long aching need. He needed to feel about her and the baby the way he felt about everyone else, not infused with some sort of mind-melding, heart-softening drug. That way he would be able to make good decisions, act responsibly.

He walked to the window and looked out at the street below. It had started to rain. Heavy clouds spewed thick drops over the passers-by below.

Finally, she came to him and made eye contact. But it wasn't what he wanted to see. All affection had gone, all excitement and hopefulness.

Somewhere along the way all his emotions had got locked up with her. Every day started and ended with thoughts of Georgie. As he turned to the window he caught sight of a stack of magazines and remembered the online dating article. She was hoping for something more.

She wanted a declaration, he supposed. Something that told her how he felt about her, about this. But he didn't know what to say. Couldn't ex-press the chaos, couldn't see through those clouds, only that his heart felt raw at the prospect of not being here. Of letting her down. But it wasn't fair to make her believe a lie.

Her voice was cold. 'And they're going to try? Is that what we've got to look forward to? You trying?'

'Surely that's better than me not trying? I'll call when I get there. I'll call as often as I can. I'm sorry it's not going to work out exactly to plan.'

'We didn't have a plan, Liam. That's just the problem. We just pretended everything would be fine, and it's not. It won't be.' She shook her head, her ponytail bobbing from side to side. She looked so young. And so cross. So magnificently annoyed. 'I won't hold my breath about the calls. I know what those satellite phones are like. You've never managed it before.'

It had never mattered so much before.

She was distancing herself from him, he could see. She was systematically putting space from her emotions, he recognised it because he'd done it himself so many times—but she never had.

When she looked back at him her resolve seemed clear. The emotions were settled, she was cold and distant. Things had irrevocably changed—including the emotions whirling in his chest like some sort of dark storm cloud, whipping away the oxygen and leaving nothing in its place. An empty chasm that hurt so hard.

He was going to help those who didn't have the wherewithal to help themselves. But, bone deep, he knew he was going because he couldn't not. Because facing other people's truths was always easier than facing up to his own. 'They need me there.'

'And we need you here.'

He looked over at the shopping bags she'd dropped on the floor. 'You bought decorations?'

'Suddenly I'm not feeling very festive. You're not going to be here.'

'I doubt it.' And that was all his fault. She'd been looking forward to spending Christmas together and he'd ruined it.

He turned to face her as hurt and pain whipped across his heart.

Her arms hugged across her chest. Her eyebrows rose as she infused her voice with a brightness she clearly didn't feel. 'So go. Save some lives. Come back safe and then be a good father to your child.'

'It'll only be for a few weeks. I'll get back for the birth. I'll make it happen.' His child. It was so close now, a few more weeks and he'd be able to hold his child.

Was that why he'd taken this job? Because he was too afraid? Was he too afraid to love his child? To love Georgie?

That idea shunted him off balance. He didn't want to look too deeply inside himself, at his motivations, so he was going by gut feeling here, because that was all he had to go on. His head wasn't making any sense. 'And what about us?'

'Oh, Liam, we want different things, I understand that now. I feel that now. I want a big messy family with two parents who love each other, with doting grandparents who want to share the joy, and you don't want any of that.' She touched her heart and a little piece of him shattered because he knew what she was saying. That this was the end. 'We just don't have the same dream.'

No. Now his heart was being ripped away. He didn't want to hear those words, to feel this hurt. But he knew that it was the only way they would ever be able to get by, to see each other and survive. Maybe one day they'd find a place where they could be friends again. 'And when I come back?'

'We'll have rewound in time to before the baby. To before you came back from Pakistan. Back to when we were just friends. When things weren't complicated. You can have your life and I'll have mine and we'll meet somehow in the middle, for this little fella. Co-parents, like we agreed.'

'But—'

'No.' Her hand flicked up to stop him speaking. 'It's what I want, Liam. What I need to get through all this. Things are going to be hard enough as they are without wondering what you want from me too, worrying if you're going to change your mind or choose something else, something more appealing. Because you do that…don't you? So it'll be better if we have no promises. No pretence. No ties between *us*. No *us*. Just this baby.'

'But—' He wanted to fight her, to fight for them, but she was right. It was easier, cleaner if they broke everything off now and got back to being friends again. If that could ever happen. Time apart would help. It had to.

'I'm used to being on my own, Liam. That way there aren't any expectations. I can't spend my life wanting people to love me if they don't. If I'm not enough, that's fine. I'll be enough for this little one.'

You're more than enough for me. For anyone. But love? That was another level he hadn't dared strive for since Lauren. Something he'd closed himself to. Love? Nah, he couldn't trust himself to go there. 'I'll be back as soon as I can. I'm sorry, about everything.'

'No. This is all my fault, Liam. I should have listened to you in the first place. It was a beyond crazy idea. And now our friendship is ruined, we can't talk without shouting. You're leaving and we're arguing. We never did this before, we used to go to the pub and give you a good send off, and off you'd trot, with a damned fine hangover, to save the world. And we cheered from the sidelines, proud and happy that you were doing something most excellent and good.

'But look at me, I'm not cheering now. I resent you for going and that's not how it should be. You'd resent me if I asked you stay. We're caught between our own needs and wants and it's too hard to live like that. Everything's changed between us. You said it would and it has. It's me who should be sorry. I made you do this. I kissed you first. I took you to my bed. I'm sorry for all of it.'

'Never. We've created something. A child. *Our* child. We can't ever be sorry for that.' He tried to pull her into his arms, to kiss her once more. To taste those honeyed lips, to feel her, soft and gorgeously round, in his arms. To feel that sense of belonging that she gave him, that reason to stay. To make him stop running from the past and look ahead to something different, something better, something not haunted by what happened before. Something more than good. But she stepped away, out of reach.

So far out of reach he didn't know if he'd ever find a way back to her.

'I need you to leave now.' She wanted him to stay. Wanted him to want to stay with her and the baby, and make a family of three. Oh, God, she wanted him. Wanted more. Wanted so much more. Wanted a different way to describe what the two of them had shared. It didn't necessarily need paperwork—she didn't expect marriage, but she did want commitment. Not just to the baby but to her. She wanted to be part of something long term. With him. She wanted her dream.

But he was running away, and he'd given her no choice in the matter.

And, yes, he'd shown commitment to the pregnancy despite her initial doubts. Not once had he wavered when even she'd had the odd wobble about impending parenthood. Hadn't he helped her create a beautiful space for her and their child? Hadn't he designed a garden? Hadn't he made sure she was safe, that she ate the right things, that his child was cocooned in the right environment to grow?

But he had still never said the word 'love' to her. Not about her or his child. Or about anyone or anything, for that matter, ever. He was all locked up in the tragedy of his baby sister and it was desperately sad but she wanted him to love someone.

She wanted him to love her.

And he couldn't. Because if he did he wouldn't be heading off on some mission that he didn't need to go on. He'd be here, holding her hand and planning a happy Christmas, supporting her in her last couple of months of pregnancy.

Was it too much to ask? Was she expecting too much?

No. It was what every couple strove for. She wanted him to feel the same way about it all as she did. She wanted him to share that excitement she felt whenever she lay in his arms. The way her heart soared when he was inside her. The sensation of utter completeness when he looked at her, when he made her laugh. She wanted him to love her and the baby the way she loved him. Wholly. Totally. Without reservation.

And there it was. The naked, ugly truth. She'd fallen in love with him.

When she should have been putting all her attention into this baby, she'd gone and fallen for its father—the wrong kind of man to love.

No.

She tried not to show her alarm and fixed her face as best as she could into an emotion-free mask as she walked away from him, while he stared at her uncomprehendingly, his hand on the doorhandle.

No. Don't go. She wanted to shout it at him. To hurl herself at him and be a barrier between him and the door. But what would be the point? Letting him go was the right thing to do. What was the point in making someone stay, hoping they would learn to love you? Hoping…

She loved him. Completely. Devastatingly. Instead of protecting herself against more heartache, she'd allowed her life to be bowled over by a man who couldn't and wouldn't ever love her. It was a simple and as difficult as that. How stupid.

And now, even worse, she was tied to him for ever. She'd insisted on that. And he'd agreed. He'd torn up the contract in a dramatic gesture of commitment and determination that had both impressed and scared her. And despite everything she knew about him, she'd believed him and somewhere deep inside a little light had fired into life and it had grown and she'd hoped…

And now the light had blown right out.

Because, after all, she'd been the silly one in all this, she'd allowed herself to dream, had allowed herself to slip under his spell, had willingly given her heart to him. He'd always been upfront. And you couldn't be more upfront than jumping on the first plane out of Dodge.

Liam had been right all along. Love could be

damned cruel. She could never let him know. 'I need you to leave. Now. I need you to go, Liam.'

'Georgie—'

'Go. I have to work.' She watched the door close behind him, and almost cried out, almost declared herself, to see if that would make a difference to him going or staying. But she wasn't about to play games, give him tests, make him say something he'd regret. Or that they'd both regret.

But, still, nothing took away from the fact that she loved him. She had probably always loved him—as a friend, as someone who she could confide in and share a joke with. He was, deep down, a good man who was conflicted, who was trying to hide from hurt, and after his experiences who could blame him? His flaws made him even more likable. Falling romantically in love with him had been the icing on the cake and she would be proud for her child to have him as a father. One day she would tell him that. When she could look him in the face again. When her heart had stopped shattering into tiny pieces.

With shaking hands she picked up her shopping bags, took out the tinsel and gaudy baubles and threw them on the table. That would be for later, for a time when she felt like celebrating. Right now Christmas loomed ahead a sad and sorry affair. A Christmas without Liam. She'd wrapped him up in her festive excitement, made him the best present a girl could have, and he'd gone. Left her, just like her mother had.

One day she'd find someone who wanted her enough to stay around.

She took a few deep breaths, swiped a hand across her face and caught a tear. And another one. Then gave up the fight and let them flow.

My God, she thought as she looked in the staff-room mirror, she needed to pull herself together; this clinic could be hard enough without the nurses falling apart too.

'Come on, girl.' Plumped up her cheeks and dried her eyes. 'There are plenty who are much worse off.' Like the people Liam was going out to save. Like the ones she had booked in now, who looked to her for support and advice. Who didn't have a healthy baby in their bellies. Who needed her dedication and attention to get them through. She allowed herself two more tears. Exactly that.

One for her, one for her baby, then she took another deep breath, put on her game face and went back out into the world.

CHAPTER ELEVEN

Two weeks ago...

LIAM LURCHED AGAINST the cold hard passenger seat as the Jeep bumped over potholes along the pitted dirt track. 'Man, these roads don't get any better. I'm going to be covered in bruises before we get to the camp.'

'Aren't you pleased to be back?' Pierre Leclerc shouted above the din of the engine, his words tinted with his French-Canadian accent and vestiges of the countless places he'd visited in his long aid career. He cracked a booming laugh and hit Liam on the thigh. 'We missed you.'

'Ah, shucks, mate, I missed you too.' Like hell he'd missed them. He'd struggled every kilometre, every minute of the interminable flight, the uncomfortable transit, the stench. The seven-day layover in Juba, getting supplies, waiting for the right documents, stuck in bureaucratic hell. The long drive out here. Every second wishing he'd had the courage to stay in Auckland with Georgie.

He just couldn't get rid of the memory of her. All grumpy and stroppy, stomping down the crowded street, the swing of her backside, the tense holding of her shoulders, the swish of her ponytail. The closed-off posture. The truth of her words. *Our friendship is ruined.* But it was all too late.

Pierre leaned across. 'I hope you bought us something decent for our Christmas stockings?'

'I have something to help us forget, if that's what you mean.' Patting his duty-free purchases of rum and whisky, he joined in the laughter, trying to be friendly, wishing like mad he was back in New Zealand, far away from this nightmare of dry earth and flies.

I made a mistake, he thought. *I made a million of them.*

They pulled into the camp compound, the dull corrugated roof of the medical building half-hidden by a layer of brown sand whipped up by the morning wind. A thin pale grey sky stretched above them, promising little relief from the scorching sun.

Liam looked around at the thousands of tents

and crudely made straw structures lining the gravel and mud path. Sun-bleached rags, tied between sticks and corrugated metal, provided the best shelter they could from relentless heat. A group of women huddled around a water tap. 'It hasn't changed at all.'

'Nothing much changes around here. It's like *Groundhog Day*.' Pierre pulled out a handkerchief and swiped it across his forehead. 'People still arrive every day seeking help, and we still struggle to house them, to feed them, to provide adequate clean water. There aren't enough toilets, the kids are all getting sick. Nothing changes at all.'

Except last time Liam couldn't wait to get here. And this time he couldn't wait to leave. 'So, what's planned for today?'

'Immunisation programme. Training the new assistants so they can go on and run it solo.'

'Okay. Let's do it.' Liam jumped down into the fog of red dust created by the Jeep wheels.

Within seconds, dozens of semi-naked children appeared screaming, laughing and singing, surrounding Liam and Pierre and clinging to their legs. Such joy in everything, even in the direst circumstances. But that was kids for you: they didn't overthink, they didn't worry or analyse, they just got on with life, running forward to the next great adventure. There was a lesson there.

Pierre steered him into the medical centre. As they squeezed past the long queue of sick people waiting to be treated Liam found himself wondering where to begin, but as always Pierre had the routine down like clockwork. And Liam easily slipped back into it.

'Okay, your turn.' He beckoned to a mother holding a small child in her arms. 'How old?'

The woman looked at him, not understanding. She offered him the child, a boy of about twelve months, scrawny and lethargic with the telltale potbelly signs of malnutrition.

'He's about one year and a half.' The base nurse translated the woman's local dialect, 'His name is Garmai. Just out of the supplementary feeding programme two weeks ago.'

Liam checked him over and measured the child's arm circumference to determine the extent of malnutrition. Garmai would probably spend the best part of his life growing up in a refugee camp, his home town too dangerous to go back to as rebels terrorised the streets and drought stole their crops.

So different from the life his own child would lead in New Zealand, where water came through invisible pipes below the ground, machines worked with the swipe of a finger and food was plentiful.

And a father half a world away.

What the hell had he been thinking?

'Eighteen months old? Really?' He spoke to the nurse. 'It looks like he still has signs of mild malnutrition. He needs to go back to the feeding centre, not stay here where he's probably only going to get sick again.'

'There isn't room. They discharged him because there's too many more coming every day.'

'They'll have to make room. This child needs help and I don't want a half-hearted effort.' He turned and smiled at the mother, trying to dredge some hope when there was little. 'I'm going to have a child. To be a father.'

He'd never given any personal information to anyone here before, not even to the staff—but the words just tumbled out. Pride laced his voice as his thoughts returned again to Georgie for the umpteenth time that day, along with the familiar sting of regret and yet startling uplift of his heart. Every thought of her brought a tumbling mish-mash of emotions and a fog of chaos. 'Soon. Very soon.'

The mother gave him a toothy grin and gabbled something to him, but a high-pitched scream grabbed their attention. A heavily pregnant woman half walked, half crawled into the room, clutching her stomach. She was immediately ushered back out and into the emergency area by two nurses.

Georgie? *Georgie.* Of course it wasn't Georgie. He'd left her to face her biggest challenge alone back at home. How would she cope with the pain of childbirth? Did she have a plan? Why the hell hadn't he made sure she had a plan? He'd phone her again, at least try to, tonight, and make sure she was okay. That was, of course, if she ever deigned to speak to him again. Her silence had been deafening.

Unlike the squawk of chattering voices and laughter and screams that filled the room as a huddle of women walked towards the emergency area. He looked up at the nurse for an explanation. 'The pregnant woman's sisters, here to help.'

'Great. She'll need some support.' He looked back at the boy, then jerked his head up again at another straggle of women walking through the room.

'The birthing attendants. The mother's mother. Her aunts.'

'Are they going to have a party or something? There's a lot of them.'

The nurse beamed. 'Of course. Family is very important here.'

As it was to Georgie. And she was going to be alone.

And that was his fault.

Watching those people come together to help their sister, to celebrate family in all its messy glory, made his heart clutch tight and he realised that Georgie had been wrong about one thing: he did want the same dream. He'd spent the last nine months trying to fight it with his head, but his hands had worked on her house, her garden, building a home for them all, a home that he loved. His arms had held the woman he adored, cradled her belly holding the baby he so desperately wanted.

For the first time in years he saw his own needs with startling clarity. He wanted to look forward instead of back. He wanted to be a father his child would be proud of. He wanted a family.

Hell, Georgie had even got him thinking about his own mother and father. And how much, deep down, he wanted to make some kind of contact with them again. He'd make a start tonight. He'd phone them and tell them they were going to be grandparents.

He wanted to be part of something good. He wanted somewhere to call home, a community of friends. Someone to love. And to be loved. The same simple dreams as every single person in this camp. He just hadn't realised it until now.

Most of all he wanted Georgie, with such a passion it stripped the air from his lungs. But he knew her heart came with a proviso. He had to love her. She wouldn't accept any less than that.

He had to love her. *Had to?* Could he do that? He sat for a moment and that thought shook through him like a physical force. He let her image fill his brain, suffuse his body with so many wild emotions. His throat filled with a raw and unfettered need.

Man, how he wanted her. He missed everything about her. He wanted her. Dreamt about her, saw her soft beautiful eyes in everyone's here, her kindness in the gentle touch of strangers, her compassion, her independence that frustrated and endeared her to him. He missed her so intensely it hurt. He needed to touch her, to lie with her, to fight with her. And, of course, to make love to her over and over and over. And such a need and such a want could only amount to one thing.

He did love her.

He'd been fighting so hard to protect himself he hadn't seen the single most important thing that had been happening.

God. He loved her and he'd walked away. No, he'd *run* away, afraid of how much she made him feel things. He'd messed up everything and now was it too late to start again? Would she even let him in the house? Would she let him love her?

Did she love him back?

He needed to know. He needed to make things right. He needed to go home.

A scream and a healthy wail echoed through the flimsy walls. New life. New beginnings. Not just for that family in there. But for him. Being here reminded him how fragile life was, and he needed to spend the rest of it with the woman he loved.

It was time to act. He needed to get back to her. Before Christmas, before the baby came. Before he lost any more time being here instead of there. He stood up and realised that a queue of people had formed, all staring at him in this tin-roofed lean-to in a place, it seemed, even God had forgotten.

Damn. He'd made too many mistakes and being here was one of them.

But how the hell to get out of this godforsaken dustbowl and bridge the fifteen thousand kilometre gap to be home in time?

Christmas Eve...

'Kate? Is that you? Hey, it's Georgie. From the clinic.' Georgie gripped the phone to her ear and tried to keep her feelings in check. This part was always the most emotional bit of her job but she wished, just this once, that she could see Kate's face when she told her the news. Knowing exactly how her patient would be feeling at this moment, she wanted to wrap her in a hug. In fact, wrapping anyone in a hug would be lovely—it felt so long since she'd done that. One month, two days and about twelve hours, to be exact. Not that she was counting.

And the loneliness was dissipating a bit now,

especially when she distracted herself. Which she felt like she had to do most minutes of most hours, because he was always on her mind. Just there. The look on his face as she'd called the whole thing off, haunting her. But it had been the right thing to do. A very right thing.

'Yes?' Kate's voice wavered. The line was crackly. 'Yes?'

'I've got the results from the blood test you came in for earlier today.'

A sharp intake of breath. 'Yes?'

'So…' Georgie read out all the numbers, knowing that this gobbledegook would mean the difference between heartache and ecstasy for this couple. 'So, all that means we have good news. Great news. You have a positive pregnancy test. Looks like you're going to have a very happy Christmas. Huge congratulations. I know how much this means to you.'

There was a slight pause then a scream. 'Oh. My God. Really? Really? Are you sure?'

Georgie couldn't help her smile. Her heart felt the fullest it had in a month. Since, exactly, the moment she'd watched Liam disappear from the clinic. 'Yes. It's very early days, obviously, and we still have to take one day at a time. But, yes, you are pregnant.'

'Oh, thank you. Thank you so much. Mark will be so thrilled. I know how much he wanted this. We both do. We can't thank you enough.'

Georgie ignored the twist in her heart at the thought of how gloriously happy this couple would be, together. Expecting a baby, making a family. Of how much Mark would be involved, and how much his love and concern for his wife always shone through his face.

It did not matter, she kept telling herself, that she was facing all this on her own. She would be fine and one day, maybe, she'd find a man who wanted her too. 'Okay, so we need to make another appointment for you for a few days' time to check the HCG levels are rising as well as we want them to, which means you'll have to come in before the New Year,' Georgie explained. 'I also need to book you an ultrasound scan…'

'Not long to go for you now?' Kate asked, after they'd finished the business end of the call. 'How are you feeling? Excited?'

'Very. There's just over a month to go and I don't feel remotely ready. I still have heaps of shopping to do, and I haven't even thought about preparing my delivery bag.'

'Get your man to spoil you rotten over the holidays, then. Make him do the fetching and carrying while you put your feet up.'

Familiar hurt rolled through her. Emails had been sporadic. Phone calls virtually non-existent. The only news she got was on the TV or radio. But even then she wished she hadn't heard anything. Too many people being killed. It was too unsafe. And all this stress just couldn't be good for the baby, so in the end she'd switched the damned TV off and played Christmas music to calm her down. 'He's overseas at the moment. I'm not sure when he'll be back.'

'That's a shame. What are your plans for Christmas?'

'Oh, just a quiet one at home.' She thought about her Christmas tree with the lavish decorations that she'd eventually found the motivation to finish last night. The small rolled turkey she'd bought and the DVDs of old Christmas movie favourites stacked up waiting for her to watch in the evenings. It was going to be an old-style Christmas, just her and Nugget. Not what she'd hoped for. And that was fine. It really was.

'Well, have a good one. *Kia kaha.*' *Stay strong.*

'Yes, thanks. Bye.' Georgie smiled as she put the phone in the cradle. Broken heart or not, she fully intended to.

Six hours later she was standing on the deck, adding the final touches to the outside decorations to the jolly and earnest accompaniment of carol singers blasting through her speakers. The deck may not have been quite finished, but the garden looked beautiful, with the candles flickering in the darkness. Liam had been right, the winery garden idea had worked well—just a shame that the edges still needed to be finished off.

But tomorrow's forecast was for sunshine and she had no intention of sitting inside when she had such a fairy-tale place to spend the day. The hammock had her name on it, along with a glass of cranberry and raspberry juice, a large helping of Christmas pudding and a damned good romance novel.

There was just one more string of lights to hitch onto a branch to make everything perfect. Standing on tiptoe, she reached up and tried to throw the lights around the branch.

Missed. *Damn.*

She tried again. Missed again. Stretching forward, she flung the lights towards the branches, the weight of her baby tummy dragging her forward and off balance.

Stepped out into…air.

She felt the scream before she heard it, rattling up through her lungs, into her throat that was filled with panic. The one single word that came to her, the only thing she wanted right now. 'Liam!'

Then she flailed around like a windmill as there was nothing and no one to stop her fall into darkness.

Now…

Pain seared up her leg with even the slightest movement. She was sure she'd broken her ankle—it was twisted at such a strange angle caught in the gap between splintered wood and the garden wall. A bad sprain anyway, too sore for her to put her weight on, and she was too wedged in to be able to lever her big fat belly upwards.

So she was stuck. *Damn.*

And hurting. *Double damn.*

And how long she'd lain here calling for help, she didn't know, but the moon was high in the sky now. Typical that she'd left her phone in the house. Typical that the neighbours had gone to their holiday home by the sea. Typical that it was Christmas and she was on her own. And the music she'd been playing seemed to be on repeat and if someone didn't turn it off soon she'd go down in history for being the first woman to have been turned clinically insane by Rudolph and his damned red nose.

And it hurt. Everything hurt. Including her heart, because she felt stupid and sad, here on Christmas Eve, alone and stuck. And for some reason her usually capable mind set had got all mushy and she felt a tear threaten. And more than anything she missed Liam.

That was it. She loved him and she missed him with every ounce of her being. And he wasn't here and he never would be. Not in the way she wanted.

She tried again to wriggle free but her ankle gave way and she didn't want to put more pressure on it. Thank God it was summer and the night was warm. At least she could be grateful for that small mercy.

No. She wasn't grateful, she was angry. With herself, with Liam, with everyone and everything. Was she going to be stuck here all damned holiday? 'Hey! Anyone? Lady with a baby here. Stuck. Help?'

Rudolph with your nose so bright...

'Shut up! Please. Someone. Help.'

Once she'd calmed down a little she tried pulling herself up again. This time she managed an inch. Two...but then nothing more. She was about to call out again when a sudden searing pain fisted across her body. And her feet got wet.

Her heart hammered just a little bit more. No. Surely not?

The baby? Now? She pressed a hand to her belly and spoke in the softest voice she could muster. 'No, Nugget! Don't you dare make your appearance here. You've got five more weeks to cook. You stay exactly where you are.'

She waited, biting back the pain from her foot. Trying not to cry. Maybe it had been a Braxton-Hicks contraction? Maybe it was all just practice?

No such luck. More pain rippled across her abdomen, sapping her breath and making her grip tight onto the side of the deck. That one had hurt. A lot. 'You are just like your father, you hear me? You have lousy timing.'

How could she have a baby here, when she couldn't even lift her leg up half an inch? Never mind that it was five weeks early. What was she going to do? Her lips began to tremble.

No. She wasn't going to cry. She was going to be fine.

More contractions rippled through her. Faster and more regular and every time they hurt just a little bit more. Time ticked on and she wanted so much to move, to free herself. To walk, to bend, to stretch.

And then more contractions came and the night got darker.

To cope with the pain she tried to conjure up an image of Liam, pretending he was here with her. Pretending he was helping her. Pretending he loved her. Because only that would be enough.

Think. Think. What could she do?

She didn't want to think. She wanted some-one to do that for her, for a change. She wanted to be tucked up in bed, her head on Liam's shoul-

der, wrapped safe in his arms. She wanted—
'Owwwww. This is all your fault, Liam MacAllister.
I hate you. I hate…*youooooww.*'

'I'm sorry. Is this not a good time?'

And now she was hallucinating, because through
all this thick soupy darkness and Rudolph on repeat and searing pain she could have sworn she'd
heard his voice.

She decided she was going to go with it. Maybe
she was already clinically insane after all. 'Yes.
You bet your damned Christmas socks it isn't a
good time. I'm caught between a deck and a hard
place. My foot's broken and I'm having your baby.'

'Right now?'

'Yes, right now.' She spoke to the Liam-shaped
smudge that appeared so real it was uncanny. And
to her endless irritation her heart did a little skipping thing. She didn't want it to skip. She wanted
it to stay angry because that was the only way she
was going to get through this. 'What the hell are
you doing here anyway? Aren't you supposed to
be healing the sick? Giving alms to the poor?'

Then he was there, really right there, with his
scent and his capable hands, and he wasn't panick-
ing like she was, he was talking to her in a sooth-

ing, very understanding voice. 'Let's get you… Oh.' His hands shoved under her armpits and he tugged. 'You're stuck.'

'Give the man a medal. Yes, I'm stuck. I've broken my ankle and Desdemona's about to make her— *Owwwwww.*' Pain ripped through her again. The contractions were coming faster now. More regular and more intense.

But he was here. Like some goddamned guardian angel, he was here. For her. He'd come back. For her?

Or was it just for the baby? She couldn't think about any of that right now. He was here.

His voice soothed over her again. 'You're going to be fine, really, but I think we need the fire brigade or someone else to help lift you out. I don't want to hurt you…'

You already have. 'No way. No way are you getting those good people out of bed on this special night just to come with their special lifting equipment and heft me out of— *Oowwwwww.*'

'Contractions are that regular, eh? We've got to get you out. How about if I…?' He put his foot against the wall and heaved her upwards, and if he hadn't been tugging at her she might have melted into his embrace just for a moment. Just held on tight, just for one solitary moment, to absorb some of his strength and his heat. Just held right on. 'Twist left a bit…wait…slowly…'

'Whoa. Watch it…' Then she was somehow shrugged up and sitting on the deck and her foot was throbbing and her stomach contracting and she gripped onto his old T-shirt while sudden enormous pain rattled through her. 'It hurts, Liam. It all hurts.'

He grimaced a little, she thought. She could just about make him out. The candles had blown out hours ago and she hadn't managed to even plug the fairy-lights in. Some other time she might have thought this was romantic. It wasn't. It hurt.

But then he pushed her hair back from her face and rubbed his thumb over her cheek and she bit her lip to stop herself from crying because he was here and she wanted him so much. But he didn't want her.

He looked right into her eyes. 'I know, darling. I know it hurts. It'll be fine. Honestly. It'll be okay.'

'No, it won't. This baby can't come yet, it doesn't have anywhere to sleep…and I haven't had my baby shower, I want my party. I want to play games—I don't want to do this.'

And I don't want you here to torment me and be the macho hero and loving father when you'll go and break my heart a million times over every time I see your face.

'This. Is. Not. My. Birth. Plan. I want gas and air. Pethidine. *Drugs.*'

'Roll with it, Geo. Looks like you're going to have a special guest of honour at that party. Because this baby is coming, whether you want it to or not. I get the feeling it has your genes when it comes to independence.'

'Oh. Oh. *Owww.*'

'Let's get you inside. It's too dark. I don't know how to help if I can't see.' Half carrying her, half walking her, he managed to get her inside and onto the lounge floor. 'The bedroom's too far. Okay. I'm calling back-up. This baby's in a hurry.'

After stabbing numbers into a phone, he rattled off information and only then did she hear the anxiety in his voice. When he turned back to her she saw him in full light. My God, he was breathtaking. But he looked concerned. No, more than that. He looked haunted. *Lauren.* 'It won't happen again, Liam. It will be fine.'

'I know, I know. Everything's okay.'

'And I think I want to push—'

Everything was not okay.

Liam consciously regulated his breathing, but there was nothing he could do about his pounding heart rate and his overwhelming sense of dread. There was every chance that this could go wrong. This was a prem scenario. The one nightmare he wanted to avoid. It was happening all over again.

He tried to shake away the image of tubes and an incubator and a tiny pink thing that grew into his crying wailing sister, but had looked so quiet and so sick that it had almost broken his heart. And of the tiny coffin that had barely filled the space in the dirt.

So, no, everything was not okay.

He inhaled sharply and took Georgie's hand and waited until she'd stopped screaming and screwing up her face. 'That's it. It's all good. You're doing well.'

How many babies had he delivered? He'd lost count. Out in the field where there was little help and lots of disease, when mum and baby had less than a good chance of surviving. And he'd never panicked. Not once. But right now he'd never wanted so much for medical equipment. For back-up. For the pain in his heart to dislodge so he could think straight. For the woman and the child he loved to be okay. 'You're doing good. Now breathe…breathe…'

At what point had he so hopelessly and completely fallen in love with her? Maybe right then that second as she stared up at him with such fear and love and relief in her eyes that it made his heart jolt. Or maybe when she'd told him to leave and he'd seen the same love shimmering in her face, even though she had been trying so hard to hide it from him. Maybe when he'd found her in the ER with a damaged eye. Or when she'd told him she was pregnant.

Or even that very first day in the sluice room ten years ago when she'd taken no nonsense and told him to harden up.

But in the last few days that thought had taken hold of him and he just couldn't shake it off. Damn fine time to realise you loved someone, right when you had a chance of losing them. But whatever happened he had to love her now, from this minute on, and protect her and care for her. And help her. And be brave for her. 'I can see the head, Geo. Breathe for me. Just a second. Breathe.'

'I don't hate you.'

A smile flowered in his heart—enough to take him past the fear and into a place of calm. They'd get through this together. 'I know. I know you don't hate me, Geo. Concentrate on the breathing.'

'Really, I'm sorry. I don't hate you—*Owwwwww.*' Then with an ear-splitting scream a slick baby slithered into his arms. The doorbell rang. Footsteps pounded into the room. Georgie cried. The baby cried. The cord was cut, a murmur of voices. A hearty chorus of congratulations!

And, able to finally breathe again, he was left staring at this miracle. His son. All ten fingers and ten toes and a hefty set of lungs. Who was managing just fine on his own. And suddenly Liam's heart was blown wide open with a different kind of emotion. A searing riotous joy and a feeling that life was just about to get gloriously messy.

Then he looked at his son's mother, who was the most red-faced, tear-stained disaster he'd ever seen. And his heart swelled some more, shifting and finding more space for love for her. And he knew in that moment that nothing would ever be the same because he'd allowed these people into his heart and that was where they were going to stay. For ever. 'You are amazing, Georgie Taylor. He is amazing.'

'It's a boy? Yes?'

'Yes. He's doing fine. Just fine.' He passed the baby to her to hold, watched as the tiny bundle nuzzled towards her nipple. 'A boy, with great instincts and a particularly well-defined MacAllister package, if I do say so myself.'

'One minute old and you're assessing his genitals?'

'It's a guy thing.' Unable to resist kissing her any longer, he lifted his head and pressed his mouth to hers. 'I love you. I love you, but I need to explain—'

'Whoa? Really? Now?' She nodded towards the team of busy paramedics. 'I've just had a baby and we have an audience, and you want to do this now?'

'Yes. Now, and always. My timing is legendary, didn't you know? I don't care who hears it, I love you, Georgie.'

Her eyes widened but she put a hand between them to create space. 'It's the hormones. You'll grow out of it in a day or two. Then you'll be hot-footing it back to South Sudan at the first opportunity.'

'No. It's taken me a decade to come to my senses, but I love you. I want to be with you. Nowhere else in the world has you, so I want to be here, to make you happy.' His throat caught a little. 'And now we have this one.'

Those wide dark eyes brimmed with tears. 'No. It's because of him that you're here. Not me. You don't love me. You want to. Oh, how you want to. But you don't.'

'Are you for real? I've called in every favour I've ever had and flown halfway across the world. Dashed straight to you. Which part of *I love you* don't you believe?'

She bit her lip and as always her stark honesty was there in her face, in her words. 'I'm scared, Liam. I want to believe it all. Wow, that would be such an awesome dream to have come true, really. I couldn't think of a better thing I could have. But you don't have to get carried away. I get that you don't like connection.'

She was rejecting him? He hadn't factored that into his plan. 'I have spent every available waking hour for the last eight months here. I have pimped your house, transformed your garden, been at your beck and call. I've been your friend through thick and thin. I am still your friend, Geo. That is the best part about all of this. We are friends first. Doesn't that prove that I love you?'

'I want your heart. Not your duty or your responsibility, or some friendship loyalty thing. I want your true love.' It was there in her face and mirrored in his heart, unfettered, truthful, raw. He needed to make her believe him. She clearly took some persuading. 'I want your true love. For me. I won't take anything less.'

'Wait. Wait right there.' He dashed out to the car, grabbed his things and dashed back. 'The paramedics are waiting outside, they want to take little Nugget—we need a name. Really, we need a name. Just to be checked out at the hospital. And to get your foot sorted. But I want to give you this first.'

He dragged the cot into the lounge and placed it next to the biggest, brightest Christmas tree loaded down with the most garish baubles he'd ever seen. 'Here. I got this.'

Her hand went to her mouth. 'You bought the cot from the French market? And you've painted it? That's very sweet, very kind of you. He'll love it. I love it.'

'And I love you. I bought this for you back then, the day after you fell in love with it. Because you wanted it so much. Because it makes you happy. I just want to do things that make you smile. I love you. Please believe me.'

'Oh, Liam.' Georgie shuffled across the sofa, trying to avoid the pain in her nether regions, her foot, and just about everywhere on her body. But it all faded just a little bit. He loved her? Did he? She'd listened out for it for so long, but he'd never used the words. She'd wanted to hear it, had waited so patiently for someone somewhere to say those three words to her. She had believed that a declaration of love could only be spoken. The deeds, though—they'd been plentiful. He'd shown her his love instead of declaring it. Every day for ten years.

For some reason she couldn't breathe, her lungs

were filled with nothing, her throat choked with a lump of emotion. 'I don't know what to say.'

'Well, don't, then. Don't say a thing. Just listen. I didn't want to fall in love because love can be damned painful. I pushed everyone away to protect myself. I didn't want a family, I didn't want those things you craved. But you've shown me how to make it work, how to take a risk. That fighting for the people you love is the most important thing of all. I love you. Because you are you. You're funny and weird and you laugh at my jokes and your smile warms my heart every time I see it. But best of all we can get through anything— hell, we've stood by each other ten years already. I'm ready for another thirty, forty, eighty... You?'

'Yes. Yes, of course.' She wrapped him into her arms, with a slight protest from the little fella. 'Thank you. Thank you so much. I love you too. Really. Truly.'

'And if you want me to give up the aid work, I will. I'll find something else.'

She shook her head. 'Enough with the crazyville talk. I know how much you need to do that work. Just maybe shorter stints? And we'll definitely discuss it, right? You won't just decide.'

'Of course not. We're in this together.' And the way he was looking at her convinced Georgie that he really did mean it. He planted a kiss on her cheeks, then laughed. 'Hey, it's Christmas Day, you realise? We'll have to think of something festive to call him. I'm sorry, but Nugget doesn't cut it.'

She looked over at the twinkling lights on the tree, at the three baubles centre stage with their names on. At the stack of DVDs and the romance novel. This was not how she'd intended spending Christmas Day, but she couldn't think of a better way. Two guys to look after. Two guys to love her. A family. A proper family—now that had always been at the top of her Christmas wish list. 'There's always Noel or Gabriel…Joseph, maybe? We could call him Joe?'

'Or…Rudolph? Rudi?'

That damned music was still playing in the background. 'Not on your life. Come here and kiss me again.'

His nose nuzzled into her hair. 'I can't think of anything else when I kiss you, my mind goes to mush.'

'That's the plan, I don't want any more suggestions like that. Besides, we've got plenty of time to think of a name, but way too many kisses to catch up on...'

He did as requested. When he pulled away it wasn't as far as he usually went. She liked that. Liked the way he was intent on staying. Liked the way he loved her.

'Happy Christmas, darling.'

'Happy Christmas, Macadoodle-doo.' She gave her man another kiss. Then snuggled into the baby snuffling in her arms. 'Happy first Christmas, Nugget.'

And many, many more to come.

* * * * *

MILLS & BOON®
Large Print Medical

July

HOW TO FIND A MAN IN FIVE DATES	Tina Beckett
BREAKING HER NO-DATING RULE	Amalie Berlin
IT HAPPENED ONE NIGHT SHIFT	Amy Andrews
TAMED BY HER ARMY DOC'S TOUCH	Lucy Ryder
A CHILD TO BIND THEM	Lucy Clark
THE BABY THAT CHANGED HER LIFE	Louisa Heaton

August

A DATE WITH HER VALENTINE DOC	Melanie Milburne
IT HAPPENED IN PARIS...	Robin Gianna
THE SHEIKH DOCTOR'S BRIDE	Meredith Webber
TEMPTATION IN PARADISE	Joanna Neil
A BABY TO HEAL THEIR HEARTS	Kate Hardy
THE SURGEON'S BABY SECRET	Amber McKenzie

September

BABY TWINS TO BIND THEM	Carol Marinelli
THE FIREFIGHTER TO HEAL HER HEART	Annie O'Neil
TORTURED BY HER TOUCH	Dianne Drake
IT HAPPENED IN VEGAS	Amy Ruttan
THE FAMILY SHE NEEDS	Sue MacKay
A FATHER FOR POPPY	Abigail Gordon

MILLS & BOON®
Large Print Medical

October

JUST ONE NIGHT?	Carol Marinelli
MEANT-TO-BE FAMILY	Marion Lennox
THE SOLDIER SHE COULD NEVER FORGET	Tina Beckett
THE DOCTOR'S REDEMPTION	Susan Carlisle
WANTED: PARENTS FOR A BABY!	Laura Iding
HIS PERFECT BRIDE?	Louisa Heaton

November

ALWAYS THE MIDWIFE	Alison Roberts
MIDWIFE'S BABY BUMP	Susanne Hampton
A KISS TO MELT HER HEART	Emily Forbes
TEMPTED BY HER ITALIAN SURGEON	Louisa George
DARING TO DATE HER EX	Annie Claydon
THE ONE MAN TO HEAL HER	Meredith Webber

December

MIDWIFE...TO MUM!	Sue MacKay
HIS BEST FRIEND'S BABY	Susan Carlisle
ITALIAN SURGEON TO THE STARS	Melanie Milburne
HER GREEK DOCTOR'S PROPOSAL	Robin Gianna
NEW YORK DOC TO BLUSHING BRIDE	Janice Lynn
STILL MARRIED TO HER EX!	Lucy Clark